CW01083110

MATT SHAW'S

CLOWN

1.

The children's screams were music to my ears. If my life had a soundtrack - such a sound would surely be the first track in the collection. Children screaming, followed by the sounds of canned laughter. I raised my white-gloved finger to my lips again and shushed them silent. The screams took a while to fade to a slight murmur. This was my favourite bit. The bit which got the biggest scream before everything finally finished. My very own encore.

I looked around the group of children sitting in front of me and reached into a large bag that I had brought with me. Their young, innocent eyes fixed upon it as they wondered what could possibly be contained within. What else had I got up my sleeve? I flashed them the biggest smile my mouth could stretch to - accentuated by the heavy red lipstick around my mouth - as I pulled out a paper plate. Keeping the smile from fading from my powdered face, I clamped my teeth around the prop before reaching back into the overly large bag. I pulled out a rubber chicken and gave it a puzzled look. I shrugged to the audience as I threw it over my shoulder. A ripple of laughter from the young crowd. I reached back into the bag and ferreted around some more. Seconds later and I pulled out an old bicycle horn. Another puzzled look in the prop's direction. It was one of those old style hooters; a trumpet with a black inflatable ball attached to the other end of it. I held it up to the face of the child I had sitting next to me on a stool we'd pulled from his mother's kitchen. Not that he could see what I was doing; his eyes were covered by my stripy scarf. I gestured to the watching children whether I should give the hooter a squeeze or not, and they all nodded frantically. Gleeful expressions on their faces. I gave them a farcical wink and went to squeeze the hooter only to stop at the last second. I turned back to my young crowd and gave them a disapproving look before sending the hooter over my shoulder and in the same direction as the rubber chicken. Back in the bag and, after another ferret around, I pulled out a can of whipped cream. This is what I had wanted. I dropped the bag onto the floor - next to my huge clown slippers - and took the plate from my mouth. I held it out and pressed the can of cream's trigger, causing a frothy mess of cream to splatter onto the plate. I kept spraying as the children watched on with amusement. They knew what was coming. At least, they thought they did. As soon as there was a mountain of fresh cream piled high enough on the paper plate, I threw the can over my shoulder in the same direction as the previously used props. I flashed them another smile as I made a gesture as though to splat the blindfolded boy in the face. They all nodded enthusiastically. Of course they did. They always did. The chance to see their friend splattered in the face with whipping cream was too good an opportunity to miss out on.

The boy in front of me was ten years old yesterday. His name was Johnny. Yesterday being a school night meant the boy's party was pushed until this afternoon. Probably for the best. Yesterday, it rained heavily for most of the day and yet today it was bright and sunny with temperatures soaring to a near-uncomfortable degree - at least uncomfortable when standing in this get-up - and the parents have decided to move the party to the garden. An act - on their part - which turns me to a smiling-on-the-inside-crying-on-the-outside kind of clown. Of course I do not say anything to them. To do so would be rude and unprofessional of me. Rude entertainers, or those who lack professionalism, do not get repeat bookings.

I waved the plate of cream in front of Johnny's face once more and - again - the audience nodded with an unrivalled enthusiasm. Their keenness at seeing their friend hit in the face with cream made me wonder whether they were really his friends at all or whether they were here for the free party bags and cake. I suppose kids will be kids. They just want to laugh.

I held up three of my gloved fingers and mouthed 'In three' at the kids.

I lowered my fingers.

I held up one finger and mouthed 'One'.

I held up a second finger and mouthed 'Two'.

I held up my third finger and mouthed 'Three'.

I raised the plate high in the air above Johnny's face and then - as planned - had it snatched from my loose grip from the boy's father. It had all been arranged at the time of booking. He wanted to be seen as The Hero of The Day, the man who stopped his son from wearing a face full of cream. The idea had come to him when he saw one of the children - at another party - get upset when he was on the receiving end of the cream splat. Johnny's father wanted to book me on the strength of that show but was worried his son would have the same reaction. To be fair, most of the children enjoyed the cream ending I lined up for them. Most of them found it funny. I'd say there were only two out of ten who didn't see the funny side. Regardless - Johnny's father wanted to spare him and asked whether he could snatch the plate from me and hit me with it instead. I didn't mind. Why would I? Still getting paid at the end of the gig. And so the plan was formulated that he'd grab the plate and splat it into my face. I'd fall over on the floor in shock whilst he took the blindfold off his son. He would then encourage his son to give me a kick up the bum as I struggled to get up, blinded by the cream. The kick was to be the final act of revenge. At that stage of the plan, I'd run from the garden - into the house - doing a comical scream; a scream I practised throughout the previous evening, much to my neighbour's annoyance.

I acted surprised when the plate was snatched from me. The look upon the children's face suggested my over-the-top melodramatic acting was absolutely spot on once again but then that's to be expected with the rate I charge. Not too expensive, but not selling myself short either. I want to entertain the children, I want them to remember their parties but, at the same time, I do have bills to pay and the cost of the various storage units is not exactly cheap.

"What are you doing?!" I asked Johnny's dad as the audience gasped. Johnny himself pulled the blindfold from his vision so he could see what was happening. Even his eyes went wide with amazement when he saw his father lean forward and slam the cream pie straight into my face. "You're ruining my show!" I shouted in an eerily high-pitched voice as I stumbled back onto my bum. I was surprised by the lack of laughter from the audience.

"It's not nice, is it?" Johnny's dad shouted at me. Again - still no laughter. I rolled around on the floor with my arms and legs flailing about. I must have looked pathetic. "Well you're not doing it to my son!" His voice changed. He initially sounded as though he were being serious, as though he were genuinely upset that I was about to playfully hit his son with a cream pie. The second line he shouted though, the bit where he said I wasn't going to do it to his boy - that was better - much more over the top. More...What was it...Cheesy. Fake. A small ripple of laughter ran through the crowd. Johnny's father noticed this too. "You're a big, fat bully!" he said. Another ripple of laughter. Louder this time. I took the opportunity to go on all fours - my big padded arse pointed to the party-goers. "And we don't like big, fat bullies, do we?" he asked the children.

"No!" they all screamed.

"Let's teach him a lesson!" Johnny's dad - the Hero of The Day - shouted. He ran up behind me and gave me a gentle kick on the bottom. I playfully screamed. "Who else wants a go?" he asked.

"ME!" several children shouted out - Johnny being one of them.

As I pretended to struggle to get up, each of the children lined up behind me and gave me a kick on the bum, their infectious laughter getting louder by the second. The perfect end to the perfect party and another satisfied customer.

"Thank you for that," Johnny's dad said as he stepped into where I was hiding in the family living room. His name was Colin. He was a tall man, fairly well built. Not the biggest of men but - even so - I'm glad he pulled the kick just a little bit. I had a feeling that had he not done so, it would have left a bruise, even with all the padding on the suit I wore. "I was worried, for a moment, that they weren't going to like the alternative ending," he said as he reached into his pocket and pulled out a white envelope. That would be my payment. What's inside, not the envelope. He handed it over to me and I slid it into the zipper pocket on the side of my yellow suit. "Think they started off thinking I was being serious," he continued. To me, this was the awkward part of the events I attended. I always found them a struggle; having to be polite to someone when all I wanted to do was put my feet up and rest a little. I'm fifty in a couple of weeks, slightly overweight (not overly so) and pretty unfit. I loved this gig. It meant the world to me but that didn't stop it from tiring me out. Can't be rude though. Need to think of repeat business. His son is ten years old. There's a chance he could want a clown at his party for at least a couple more years yet.

"I think they loved it," I forced out. "My bum - not so much," I laughed. Had Colin known me, he might have known the laugh wasn't a genuine one. Again, laughing on the outside and crying on the inside.

"Well, thank you again. I've slipped a little extra something into the envelope for you as an additional thank you," he smiled and winked at me. It was always good when they felt the necessity to tip and - thankfully - most of them did. But then, I did always give one hundred and ten percent to the shows I put on. For a reasonable rate they got balloon animals, dancing, silly walk competitions, animal impressions and anything else I could think of. Most of my routines were the same for each party; I tended to keep the same order of events too. Why change a winning formula? Even the cream pie ending. The kids would sit there on their chairs, blindfolded, but they knew what was coming. I think the anticipation was half of the fun for them. Well - usually. Like I said - two out of ten kids weren't as keen on the act but you can't win them all and I tended to try and make amends with them by letting them get me back with their very own cream pie. Fair is fair after all and I hated to leave on a sour note.

"Thank you, but you didn't have to," I said.

"Listen - if you want - you can use one of the rooms upstairs to get changed in? Must be boiling in that get-up."

"It's fine, thank you. Used to it now," I laughed. "Right. Unless there's anything else I can do for you, I'll slip out now."

"They're just cutting the cake up now and then I think we're more or less finished for another year. Unless you wanted some cake?"

I struggled to get out of the seat. Had to stand up. If I'd stayed there much longer, chances are I'd have fallen asleep. The effort taken to perform such a show, especially in this heat, sure does take it out of you. "I'm good, thank you. But - listen - it's been fun."

Colin extended his hand to me and I took it in my own. We shook and I picked up my bag of props; pretty sure I have it all.

"It was great. I can't thank you enough..."

"Well if you know of anyone in need of a clown..."

"...I'll be sure to recommend."

"That's all I ask," I replied as he walked me through to the front door. He opened it and I carefully stepped out. There was only one step down to the driveway but - in these shoes - that's sometimes enough to send me flying to the floor in a crumpled heap. Been doing this gig for so many years and still get caught out from time to time. And the problem is - when you do fall - people think you're joking around, what with being dressed as a clown. They just clap and cheer. A free laugh at my unplanned expense.

I made my way down the drive and onto the road where my van was parked up. A white van with my working name etched down the side of it along with a generic picture of a clown. Nothing fancy. It gets me from A to B and that's all I care about. People don't hire me for my van - just my prat falls and silly antics. I kicked the over-sized shoes off my feet so I was barefoot and jumped into the van. I threw my bag of props across to the passenger seat, along with the shoes. They slumped off and landed in the footwell. I leaned back in the comfortable seat and sighed. A quick moment to catch my breath before I slid my white gloves off and tossed them to the side too. Sweaty hands wiped down the front of the already dirty clown outfit. Guess I'll have to wash that when I get in. A shame, considering how tired I am. Sometimes I go home full of energy and other times I go home with the distinct feeling of being too old for this, part of me contemplating finding something else to do for the remaining years of 'work' I have left. But what does a retired clown do once he hangs up the big, red nose? I guess I could always work in a joke shop, or something similar. Maybe a fancy dress store? I shuddered at the prospect of getting a steady nine to five job as I slid the van's key into the well-scratched ignition. A quick twist and the old girl spluttered into life, coughing a thick plume of black smoke from the rear exhaust. Had I charged a little more for the services I provided, I may have been able to get her fixed or replaced depending on costs.

I crunched my way into first gear and pressed my foot on the accelerator. At least I'll be home soon with an evening to myself before tomorrow's appointment. Funny how it goes. You can go for ages without a single hint of a booking, using more and more of your savings with each passing day and then - suddenly - they all come along at once. Johnny was my third booking this month. Tomorrow's booking makes four and - more importantly - the least amount of money needed to ensure all bills are paid. Well, all bills are paid so long as I have a bit of a fiddle on the taxes. As I approach sixty, I guess it's fair to say I'll never be a rich man unless I win on a lottery ticket but to do that I might have to start buying them. It was a good thing I didn't do this job for the money.

It was never about making money.

It was only about bringing joy to the lives of the children I met.

II

My house was as quiet as it always was. Sometimes this was a blessing and sometimes it felt as though it were a curse. Just me bouncing off the walls of the modestly-sized building that was only mine due to a generous last will and testament. I threw the clown shoes and bag of mixed props into the corner of the hallway. One perk of living alone is the fact I do not have anyone due to come home who'll moan at me for not putting things away properly. I unzipped the front of the clown suit via a small, concealed zipper which ran from neck line down to belly and slipped it off my shoulders down to my waist, instantly refreshed by the cool breeze blowing in through the house due to the windows left open. In this day and age not many people are comfortable leaving their windows open but I have nothing to lose. Not a lot in here for anyone to steal. At least - nothing that's of any worth. Hell, I don't even have a flat screen television, just some old, dated set that can't even receive the signal for digital transmissions. Not that there is anything worth watching upon the channels missing. Just depressing news stories about crimes; murders, government conspiracies, missing children - always the same.

I pulled the green wig from my head and felt instant relief. All these years wearing the damned thing, you'd have thought I would be used to it by now but it still itches like crazy. Had I had more hair, I'd have just dyed that green. I threw the wig onto the stairs so I knew where to find it the following day. By the time I walked down the hallway and into the kitchen, I had more or less stepped out of my outfit completely.

Just the make-up on and the red nose (which surprisingly isn't as uncomfortable as you'd imagine). I pulled the nose off and threw it over my shoulder, back down the hallway, and walked over to the washing machine. Supposed to hand wash this but I have to be honest - I can't be bothered and the washing machine hasn't done any damage to it after all these years so...Why stop? I slammed the door shut and set it up for a quick wash. Not enough time for a full wash; not if I wanted it to be dry in time for tomorrow's booking.

And now - now I could take the time to relax. I walked through to the living room and dropped down onto the sofa. My reflection stared back at me in the television screen. I was still wearing the white powder upon my face. I rarely take that off. I don't like the face underneath. I don't like the person underneath. I find him hard to control. I find him hard to talk to. I find him hard to keep quiet. The make-up I wear keeps him hidden. The make-up keeps him at bay and that's the way I like him. I reached for the television controller and hit the little red button. The screen buzzed into life. A second later and sound came from the small speakers. A button press on a second controller, next to where I sat, and my small DVD unit spun into life. I'm not really a film person. I do not like the violence and unnecessary bad language. The only disks in my collection are old movies featuring Laurel and Hardy - the best comedy double act of all time in my humble opinion. They don't make them like this anymore. The film's production company blurred its way onto the screen and was soon replaced with the main title of the film. I settled back in my chair and reached for a lever tucked between my sofa's padding and its arm. A quick pull and it activated the foot rest. That's better. I knew I wouldn't see the whole movie. My eyes were already feeling heavy but it didn't matter. I had seen it more times than I could remember.

"Wake up."

I opened my eyes. I hadn't even been asleep. I was merely resting my eyes for a moment.

"Look at you. You look a state. You let Laurel and Hardy see you like this? You're a fucking disgrace."

"Shut up. You aren't here."

"Yes, I am. Doesn't matter how many layers of fake you bury me under. I'm always here."

"No. You're not."

"This out-of-sight-out-of-mind bullshit you're running with...It doesn't work. You know it doesn't work. Stand up."

"I don't want to."

"Stand the fuck up, cunt!"

I can't afford to anger him so I pulled myself to my feet.

"Go to the bathroom."

"Please...I just want to relax. I just want to watch my programmes."

"We have work to do. Go to the bathroom. You need to see this."

"I don't want to."

"I will hurt you."

I walked through to the downstairs bathroom, a small room to the side of the front door - a room I purposefully kept shut.

"Please, I don't want to go in there."

"Quit being a little bitch and get in there!"

I opened the door with my hand shaking. A slight hesitation and I stepped into the room.

"Look in the mirror."

"I don't want..."

"Look in that fucking mirror."

I turned to the wall adjacent to the door. Hanging on the wall was a small mirror. I caught sight of my reflection within its tiny frame: five foot nine - fairly stocky (sadly not muscle), balding, hardly an oil-painting despite the layers of powder and paint upon my face, slight facial hair - not quite stubble and yet not quite a beard (currently covered by white). I smiled at myself.

"See. Doesn't matter how much shit you put on me, I'm still here. I'm always here and you need to get that in your goddamned head once and for all. You understand me? We have work to do."

Another flash of my pearly whites and a wink.

2.

I smiled as the front door opened. The shock on the lady's face suggested she wasn't the one who had booked me.

"One for you," I said as I handed her one of the balloons in my hand. I always turned up to parties with a large bunch of balloons. I always found it a good ice-breaker: turn up, enter the room where the party was happening, hand out the balloons to the children (and sometimes the parents). From there I'd go onto making balloon animals. I say animals plural but there were only ever a couple of choices and - even then - I tended to opt for the simple choices such as 'dog'.

The lady took the balloon from me, a confused look upon her face. I started to worry that I had the wrong house. I'd never done this before - gotten the wrong house - but I guess there is a first for everything. And after the poor night's sleep I had last night, it wouldn't surprise me if today was the 'first'.

"I'm sorry..." the lady said...

Here we go...I have the wrong house. How embarrassing.

"...I think there has been some kind of unfortunate mix-up."

Okay. Wasn't expecting that.

A man appeared behind her.

"Oh shit," he said. He looked sheepish. I could already tell I wasn't going to like where this was headed. "You didn't get my message?"

"What message?" I asked. I never switch my mobile off. I never have it more than a few feet from where I am. When you're self-employed, such as I am, you know the importance of keeping it close by as you do not want to miss any potential business opportunities.

"Our son changed his mind..."

"Changed his mind? What? He doesn't want a birthday party?" I could hear children laughing and screeching in the background. Clearly there was a party taking place within the suburban home. I peered around the front porch and in through the living room window. There are about twenty children in there.

"He didn't want a clown," the man said. I forget his name but I'm pretty sure we spoke before on the telephone; when he was booking the party. He didn't cancel it. He hadn't tried calling me. Even if he had, there would have been a missed call on my phone, something to suggest he'd attempted to contact me. But there was nothing. I wanted to stand here and argue with the (I presume) father but it wouldn't serve any purpose. He didn't want me there. There was nothing else to it. Arguing on the doorstep wasn't going to change that. "Here," the man held out a ten pound note, "for your troubles..."

The temptation was to take the money but I didn't. I didn't think it would give a good message to prospective customers. After all, mix-ups happen. "Keep it," I said. I turned away from him and started off down the drive. I stopped and turned back to the man and woman, "Just one thing...What did he choose?" There weren't many more people in this small town who offered entertainment at children's parties, so it sounded as though there was some more competition to contend with, not that competition is necessarily a bad thing.

"Iron Man," the man said.

Iron Man? I had another look in through the living room window. Standing in front of the children, in what appeared to be a second-rate outfit, was a knock-off Iron Man. Going by the screams from the house - doesn't look as though the kids cared.

"Did you want your balloon back?" the lady asked from the doorway.

I turned away from the window. "No, you can keep it," I said as I walked back to my tired, old van, a distinct feeling of 'hurt' running through me. It wasn't the fact that I had been ousted from a job; after all, there was no sense being there if the child yearned for something else. It was more to do with the fact I wasn't even worth a phone call. Sure, he said he had phoned but he didn't. He couldn't have. Could he? Maybe my phone was broken.

Back in the van (shoes off), I pulled my mobile from my pocket and dialled through for any possible voice messages. Just as I suspected there weren't any new or saved.

"What did you expect?"

"Please leave me alone, I'm not in the mood."

He was staring at me in the rear-view mirror of the car. What he had said the previous night, he was right; he was always there, despite trying to hide me underneath the make-up. He was always there waiting to taunt me, waiting to upset me, waiting to make me do those things he kept whispering to me during the night.

"You pride yourself in being a professional."

"There's nothing wrong with that."

"Not necessarily. In any other job. But do you honestly expect people to take you - us - seriously wearing that? Look at yourself. Look at what you've become throughout the years. A laughing stock."

"I'm supposed to be, it's my job."

"You know what I mean. No one takes you seriously. They treat you like the fool that you are."

"What does it matter to you?"

"Because they do the same to me."

I shifted in my seat uncomfortably. He hated the fact I did this for a living. He believed children should be seen and not heard. Or - better yet - neither seen nor heard.

I argued with him for many years before I turned to this; my argument being that there is no better sound in the world than the sound of children screaming with delight. Joyous laughing is infectious and you can't help but feel it with them. The smell lingering in the van from a late night drive last night reminded me of his stance on the subject. I tried to stop him - of course I did - but he didn't listen. He never did. Just called me a pussy and made me take a hold the knife.

He continued, "Walking around the town pretending to be everyone's friend. Volunteering to help out at charity events - these people are laughing at you and not in a way you're trying for," he hissed.

"You're wrong."

"I'm not. And you know it. You can see it in their eyes, just as you think you can see the evil in mine. But of course you won't listen to me. You'll just try and bury me under any layer of shit. Fucking pathetic."

"You're wrong," I repeated once more.

"Of course I am. I am always wrong. You're right. I'm wrong."

"Please. Why can't you just leave me alone?"

"What are you going to do with the rest of your day then?" he asked, clearly ignoring my pleas. "What else have you planned now this gig has fallen through?" He was sneering at me, his top lip curled up. "Hey! I know, why don't we go to the park and put a free show on for the darling little children?" He was mocking me.

On the warmer weekends - such as this - I did go down to the town's park, a large grassy area with a playground and small cafe area. It was always so busy down there with the families making the most of the sunlight. I didn't mind working for free, going around and making them laugh with various antics but it was a good place to network. The amount of business I had got from working the park. So - in answer to his question - yes I probably would go to the park and work the crowds. After all, I was already dressed up. And it meant the delay in taking the mask off. Keep this mask on for as long as I can.

He laughed, "You realise the mask doesn't make a difference. I'm still here…"

"It does."

I punched the rear-view mirror knocking it off-centre. Can't see my reflection here. I breathed a sigh of relief as I fired the van up. Another splutter of smoke hacked from out the back. Had the gig not been cancelled this month, I might have had enough left over from paying the bills to get the van seen to. I guess that's out of the window now. A quick check over my right shoulder to check the road for oncoming traffic. The road was clear and I pulled out.

"So - are we going to the park?"

II

By the time I got to the park, and found a space for the van in the overcrowded car park, he had gone quiet. Thankfully so. His incessant talking was getting to me. Over the last few days, maybe even weeks, he had been getting louder. It wasn't just his voice which disturbed me. I knew he had been going out at night too, whilst I slept, taking the opportunity whilst I rested to take the van and head to wherever he chose to go during the twilight hours. I don't want to know where he goes and so I've never asked him. What I don't know can't kill me.

I swung my bare feet from the van and sat there for a moment, perched on the edge of the driver's seat, looking out at the rolling fields of the park before me. Just as had been suspected, the fields were littered with people of varied ages. From the comfort of the van, I could see some of them were merely walking hand in hand, others were walking with their pet dogs on long leads, some were kicking a ball around, whilst others were watching their children play in the park's playground (behind a fence near the park's entrance).

The sun on my heavily made-up face feels nice. Would give anything to rest up now and just sunbathe along with everyone else but that doesn't get the bills paid. Being self-employed, you find you need to keep working. You need to keep yourself visible to potential customers. You need to keep networking. People think my job is easy - the amount of people who've made such comments at the end of one of my gigs. I'd love to see them slip the shoes on, and the outfit - especially on hot days - just to see how they fare. My shows usually last for about an hour. I reckon - these people - they wouldn't last twenty minutes. And even if they did, I'll wager they're incapable of raising a laugh from the crowds watching.

I shut my eyes a second, enjoying the sun beating down upon me. Could stay here all day but it won't do. I opened my eyes and leaned back into my van towards the passenger side where I'd earlier thrown the oversized shoes. I pulled them out and dropped them onto the floor, next to where I was perched in the van. Before I slid into them (and it really is a question of sliding into them), I reached back to the passenger side and grabbed the large fabric bag of props. To be honest, I'll probably not need this today. A day like this, an audience who can freely come and come…I'll most likely end up just doing balloon animals. Balloon tricks always pull in the crowds. And - when the kids leave the impromptu show with a new 'toy' - it means they're more likely to remember me when they get home. The balloon gimmicks are quickly forgotten by the parents but the smiles on their kids' faces aren't as easy to forget and before you know it, I'll have a booking (or two).

I stepped into the shoes and bent down to do them up. As I was tying the laces, I could already hear people had spotted me: a buzz of excitement bouncing from the corners of the car park from the children who'd spotted me; a feeling of 'money slipping through finger tips' at the thought of having to spend money on whatever they believe I am offering. The fact I'll charge for nothing will come as a nice surprise to them.

I closed the door of the van and locked it up before sliding the key into my pocket.

Here we go.

Show time.

III

It wasn't a complete waste of my Sunday. The odd balloon animal here and the odd balloon animal there. Smiles on the faces of the few people who did stop to watch me, which was nice, but a feeling I'd earlier felt at the lost gig as more and more families walked on by me without so much of a backward glance; the desperate feeling of losing my audience. First they're stolen away by a fake Iron Man and then they're stolen away by the lure of...What...Kicking a ball around a park or swinging backwards and forwards on a swing? Both things they could do at anytime. How often did they get to see someone such as myself perform for them?

Usually, a day of performing in the park - or even the town centre - would see me give out more than a dozen business cards; nothing fancy, just a card with a picture of balloons and my phone number. I always meant to get the cards updated, so they looked a little more appealing, but it just never seemed to happen. After a day like this, I'm not even sure if it is worth getting them updated. Maybe I should re-think what I do? Invest the money in fake Iron Man suits, or something similar. When I started, there were superheroes around but they never seemed to be popular for children's parties. Clowns, though, were in great demand. But as the years have gone on, that demand has dwindled. It kind of makes me wish I had purchased superhero outfits before they became popular and the price trebled.

Shoes thrown in the corner of the hallway, green wig dropped on the stairs. I was lying on the bed staring at the ceiling, fully dressed because I couldn't be bothered to change from my clothes. I'm so very tired. Felt tired all day. Rough night I guess, although I don't remember stirring. I remember talking to him and going up to bed. Soon as my head hit the pillow, I was out like a light. I don't know, maybe I'm coming down with something? Either that, or age is squeezing the energy from my body as the years continue to slip on past me at a rate faster than I'd like to acknowledge. It probably doesn't help that I've not eaten anything today other than an ice cream I bought from the van parked up in the middle of the park. Can't be bothered to cook now, just want to sleep forever. So tired. Don't even remember leaving the park.

3.

I hate him. Whiny, pathetic, little runt. A cunt. Always bleating on about his love for the children. Oh it's their screams of delight that drive me. The sound of their laughter is like music to my ears. He's in his fifties; deaf cunt wouldn't know music if a monkey hit him over the head with a frying pan all the time a tune was belting out at maximum speed. He makes me sick. Ashamed to think of him as my housemate. How he even made it this far in life is beyond me. He should have just been drowned at birth by his whore mother and alcoholic father.

"Don't worry, honey, we'll get it right the next time," the drunk father could have been heard to say as he held what he perceived to be the bastard child under the shallow water of the bathtub. Drink it, you little fucker, drink it until you breathe no more. Although if that were the way his life started I'm not sure where that would have left me. I don't know - maybe I would have found a home with someone else? Thinking about it now and that doesn't sound as though it would have been bad. Certainly couldn't have been any worse than where I am now. Stuck in here, with him. The cunt. His drive to do what he does - despite the knowledge it cannot and will not last forever - annoys me more than words can say. If the overly large shoe were on the other foot, I'm sure he'd be saying the same about me. But would he? The pussy rarely speaks out. He does all he can to avoid confrontation. He believes it isn't professional. He believes it will harm his business. Someone queue jumps him in a queue for groceries, he tells them not to worry about it and the next thing we know, he is letting more people past him because he 'has all day'. Someone pushes past you in a queue, you should take that position back. I've told him this. Not just once but on many occasions. He doesn't listen though. Never does. He either pretends he hasn't heard me or he argues the toss with me. By the time we have finished having a back and forth, the person who needs to be moved back to the rear of the queue has not only left the shop but also loaded their transport and driven from the store's car park.

I stand by what I've told him before - he is the laughing stock of the town but not in the way he hopes, or argues, for. It isn't because of the outfit he wears or the acts he performs. He raises a smile, and a laugh, because of his pathetic nature.

And that's why I need to restore the balance whenever the opportunity presents itself.

Like tonight.

II

I borrowed his van. I never ask for permission and I presume he doesn't mind. He never says anything to stop me so if he does have a problem, until he is man enough to deal with it face to face with me I'll continue to take it. He should just be thankful that I at least replace the fuel that I use so it's not all coming out of his tiny wage.

I do not enjoy driving around in his clapped out banger of a vehicle. The bad paint job, the stuttering engine hacking out plumes of black smoke upon start up - it's an embarrassment but still better than walking. We've had the conversation about changing vehicles in the past but it always ends the same way; he needs it for his work. I can't exactly go out and trade it in against a new model - more's the pity. I think if I were to do that, it could well be the final straw for us. A fragile friendship pushed to breaking point. Loves this fucking van as much as he loves children.

I don't know - part of me thinks I'm going to wake up one day and find his name on some kind of sex register, not that I get to see the news very often. He doesn't like reading or watching TV, so that means I don't get to read or watch, either.

"Well, officer, he told me he loved children but I never thought he meant like that..." Of course I'd plead ignorance. No way I want to go down with him. I know what they do to perverts in prison and that's definitely not for me.

I turned down a quiet alleyway which was only just wide enough to fit the van down, as made evident by the fact I clipped the wing mirror turning in. I'm sure he won't mind. State of the fucking van, I'm sure he won't even realise.

My mind keeps coming back to his cancelled party and the poor show he had in the park; if this carries on, I wonder if it means he will start to see the world the way I see it or whether he'll just throw himself into denial even more? It would be great if he didn't feel the need to hide himself behind make-up. Great if he'd grow a pair of balls and quit being such a fucking pussy. I don't know. Knowing my luck he will most likely ruin it for the pair of us and end up doing something stupid like blowing his brains out or hanging himself from one of the rafters in our home. Mind you, if he gets down that route, he'll have to lose some weight first. Fat cunt will most likely snap the fucking rafter. But then maybe that's what he needs? A close call with death to show him how much he wants to actually live? Perhaps I could set something up for him? No. I can't. Knowing my luck he won't stop me and I'll end up killing him. Major backfire.

I think half the problem with him is because he enjoys dressing up as a clown. He pretends he doesn't do - I don't know - I think he does. After all, why else would you continue doing it, especially when no one really respects you? He pretends it is all about the parties and the entertaining but that's a thinly-veiled lie. He enjoys dressing up because it gives him a chance to hide who he is. He thinks I do not know this but I do. I think that, if he were not able to wear such an outfit anymore, he might just start to realise who he really is and what is really important to him. He'll come to terms with all of that and what he really wants to do with his life. This would be great for me because - if he were to do that - well, we both want the same thing.

A check in the rear-view mirror, straightened up after his earlier pathetic outburst, and I was clear from people following me. I killed the van's lights, plunging us into near darkness thanks to the lack of street lamps down this particular alley, an alley chosen for this very reason along with the fact it was pretty isolated from the main part of the town where the nightclub boys and girls may still be milling about. I opened the door and jumped on down from the driver's seat. I left the engine running so as not to have to endure the loud backfire when the time comes to start it back up again.

I walked to the back of the van and opened it up. The smell hit me more or less straight away. Leaving this in here during the hot day clearly had not done anything for its freshness. I reached in and took a hold of the black bin liner with a white gloved hand (courtesy of borrowing part of his uniform). As I pulled the bag from the van, a little liquid leaked from a small hole in the bottom of it. My fault. I should have double bagged it. It was obvious the weight was going to be too much for the one bag. I dropped it to the floor with a dull thud and looked back to a dumpster I had seen as I drove down the alley - a large metal can with a lid tucked into the back doorway of what looked to be a Chinese restaurant. I walked over to the dumpster and lifted the not-so-heavy lid. Fucking smell of rotten chicken and other meats hit me. Jesus. Should have brought a fucking nose-peg with me. I lifted the first few bags from the top and put them on the floor before walking back for my own bag. I lifted it and reached under to hold it from beneath. Don't need the bag splitting all the way.

I staggered it over to the dumpster and lifted it to the edge of the opening. A second later, to catch my breath, and I pushed it in. Easier than I imagined. I picked the bags up from the floor and buried my own bag with them. The fucking smell of this dumpster, I couldn't have picked a better place to dump my bag. The sheer stink of this dumpster - no one is going to go ferreting around in it. I slammed the lid shut and returned to my van. Despite the problems I'm having at home - with him - I'm feeling good. I always am when I dump the bags off. It's like a heavy weight lifted from my shoulders.

I leaned down to the radio and turned the dial. Music crackled through the damaged speakers. I half-expected it to be some kind of carnival music, given the look of the van and my 'sometimes' friend's like for all things 'clown'. Thankfully, it was a standard radio channel - some presenters talking about this and that. Sure I'll pick it up the more I listen and - until then - I do not care. Homeward bound.

III

I stepped into the shared home and quietly closed the door so as not to wake him up. I don't want the hassle of having to explain where I've been this evening. He's always so paranoid that I've been up to no good and it doesn't matter what I say to try and appease him; he never believes anything I have to say. I can't say I blame him, given the fact we both know what I've been doing all night. I say we 'both' know but he never admits it to me; never lets on he knows what I get up to when the sun goes down and the cover of the night hides my movements.

I crept through to the kitchen and dropped the white gloves on top of the rest of the outfit. He'd come in from the park and thrown it in front of the washing machine. Not sure why he didn't just put it in the washing machine. Probably testing me. Probably wanting to know how long it will be before I put it in there for him. Well - he has a long wait. I'm not his bitch. If anyone is the bitch - he is mine. I froze as I noticed a tiny speck of red on the white fabric of the glove. It's not massive but I noticed it and that meant there was a good chance he would too. I can almost hear the conversation now, quizzing me over what I'd been using his gloves for. Of course I'd deny touching them at all and try and make him believe it was him who had tainted them. What's the point? It would only cause an argument.

I bent down and scooped the outfit up before throwing it into the washing machine.

He'd best not get used to it.

I slammed the washing machine's door shut and turned the machine on.

"What are you doing?"

My heart skipped a beat. Didn't even hear the bastard coming. Rare for him to make me jump. Usually it is the other way round.

"I'm doing you a favour. Would it hurt you to say thank you?"

"You? Doing me a favour? Why am I suddenly suspicious?"

"If you want, I can turn it off and let you do it yourself?"

"No. It's fine. Just you don't usually..."

"Next time I won't bother. That suit you better?"

"I'm sorry. Didn't know you were down here anyway. I only came down for a glass of water."

I didn't respond. He'd fucked me off. Regardless of why I really put the stuff in the washing machine, the fact is I put it in the washing machine. I saved him from having to do it. He should have just said thank you but - no - he has to question my intentions. He has to be suspicious as to my motives. I'm sick of him looking down his nose at me as though he's the better person. How he can believe anyone to be better than him - knowing he dresses as a fucking clown for the living - is beyond me. He is the bottom of the food chain. He just doesn't realise it.

I watched as he poured himself a glass of water. He thinks I am the selfish one and yet he didn't even bother to offer me one. No that's fine, mate, you just do whatever you want. Never mind what I may or may not want. Still waiting for my thank you.

"What have you been doing?" he asked me. There he goes again, being suspicious.

I watched him take a sip from his cool glass of water.

"Wouldn't you rather know what I am doing?"

"Do I want to know?"

"Try me."

"Okay - what are you doing?"

"Oh, nothing, just standing around here waiting for some fucking thanks."

I leaned down and turned the washing machine back off again. If he can't even say thank you to me, he can do the fucking thing himself. Before he had the chance to say anything I stormed off, leaving him to it. Even if he did say a thank you now, it would only be because I brought it up. I don't want some afterthought thank you. A pathetic token gesture of thanks. No. I'm better than that. I'm worth more than that.

Fuck him.

IV

The reaction was typical of him. To be fair, I'm so tired still that saying thank you didn't even cross my mind. Definitely have the feeling I am coming down with something. It's like I've been running around all night even though I've been up there sleeping in the comfort of my bed. Glad I don't have any bookings this week. At least, glad in so much as I don't have to get up in the morning. Can stay in bed and try and sleep this bug off.

I leaned down and flicked the washing machine back on. It started through with its spin cycle as I walked back over to the kitchen sink. A twist of the cold tap and I re-filled the glass. I walked back up the stairs towards my bedroom. I put the cup of water on the side and collapsed onto the already ruffled duvet. Can't believe it's so cold already. I've only just gone downstairs and yet it feels like I've never been in here. I pulled the cover over myself and shut my eyes.

I'm tired and yet my brain feels more awake than it has felt for these past few months. What was he doing up at night? What was he doing in the kitchen? Usually he doesn't disturb me. I very rarely hear him moving around at night even when I know for definite he has been up and about. I come downstairs and things have been moved from where I had left them. Never really know for sure what he does at night and pretty sure I wouldn't want to know. Not going by some of the things he whispers to me when we're at the parties. He's a monster.

I twisted and turned as I struggled to get comfortable, troubled by thoughts of what he had done, or had been doing. For all I knew, I was making a mountain out of a molehill but I didn't know for sure and it was impossible to ask him outright after he stormed off leaving me on my own. Funny - normally I want nothing more than for him to leave me be. The one time I want him here, he isn't around.

"I am here."

"I thought you'd left?"

"Where would I go?"

To Hell.

"What were you doing tonight?" I asked him.

"A favour for you."

"Before that," I continued to push him.

"Why don't you let me show you?"

"Just tell me."

"No. I want to show you."

"I'm not sure I want to see."

"You're ready to see it."

"Not sure that I am."

"Let me show you. I'll even walk you through it - step by step. It'll be a good chance for us to bond."

"I'm not…"

"Stop being a fucking pussy, you snivelling piece of shit. Get out of bed and come with me."

My heart skipped a beat at the sudden aggression. I should have known it was coming. It didn't matter how a conversation started with him it always ended with the same amount of aggression. The anger and hostility coming - usually - from him not getting his own way.

I threw the covers off and slowly climbed out of bed.

"Yes, that's it," he sneered. "Grow a pair of balls." He laughed. "You need to put your shoes on. We're going out," he continued.

"Where are we going?"

"Hurry up. We don't have much time left before the sun will start to come up."

"Just tell me where we're going."

"I can't. You need to see for yourself. Trust me; I think it will be good for you."

I felt uncomfortable. I was the one who usually kept the control. I was the one who decided what we did and didn't do together and yet here he was, dictating to me what was to be done. It didn't feel right. I didn't like the feeling of not being in control. Just to get to the end of the evening though - and find out what he did - I walked from the bedroom, down the stairs and to where I'd kicked my shoes off earlier. I slid them on and tied the laces as he watched. I could hear him breathing. He sounded excited. A feeling of dread washed through me. Where were we going?

4.

I watched as he drove my van. He seemed at ease behind the wheel which didn't surprise me. Had he not driven it before, he'd have probably been a little nervous about driving it. It was, after all, quite a bit bigger than a car - the sort he'd possibly be used to driving. He'd driven it before, though, despite his protests. I'd get in after a good night's sleep and the driving position would have changed. Or I'd go to get the keys from where I'd left them and they wouldn't be hanging there - or they wouldn't be hanging on the exact peg I'd left them on. It was the little things, the little details he thought I didn't notice but I did. I always noticed.

"Where are we going?" I asked him again.

"You'll see," he said.

"Can't you just tell me?"

"Even if I did, you wouldn't be any the wiser. You need to see for yourself."

I looked out of the window and didn't recognise where we were and yet there was a strange feeling that I should have known. I was sure I hadn't been there before, yet...A nagging doubt in the back of my mind that I had. It was weird. We turned down another unknown-to-me road. I wasn't sure where he was taking me and yet I already knew I wasn't going to like it. The fact he wasn't telling me where we were going - keeping it secret - just made me feel that little more uneasy about it all.

"How far is it?" I asked him.

"We're nearly there," he said. His eye caught mine via the rear-view mirror. There was a glint there which cemented my feeling of uneasiness.

"How'd you even find this place?" I asked him as he turned the van down another quiet road.

"Exploration."

"What were you even doing out here?" I asked.

He turned the van down a tight alleyway, clipping the wing-mirror in the process. I stared at the rear-view mirror in the hope he'd see my disapproving look. He didn't.

"Well," he said. He pulled the van to a stop with a judder.

"What? We're here? There's nothing here.'

"You wanted to know where I went this evening - get out."

"Is this where you drive off?"

"Don't tempt me."

I opened the van door, as did he, and climbed out. I closed the door.

"This way," he said. He walked us to a dumpster.

"What is this?"

"This is a dumpster," he said.

"I don't understand."

"Of course you don't. Open it."

I looked at the dumpster. Even from here - a few feet away - I could smell it. The contents, whatever they were, were clearly rotting. Hardly surprising given the daytime temperatures recently.

"Open it," he repeated, his voice showing a brewing irritation.

I hesitated. "Not sure I want to," I told him.

He sighed. "Are you ever going to grow any fucking balls?" he hissed.

"It's a bin. You want me to go rooting around in the bin?"

"Sooner rather than later, if you could. Day is coming."

"Look - it's not my business what you do in the evening. If you're happy - it's fine...I'm sorry, I shouldn't have stuck my nose in..."

"Open the fucking dumpster. You need to see this. It will do you some good. It'll make you realise what you need to do with your own life."

"I just..."

"Get the fuck out of the way."

II

I pushed him out of the way. He didn't take much to move. He was just standing there, watching, as I stormed over to the dumpster. Fucking stinks. I lifted the lid and pulled out the first few bags - the ones I'd used to bury the bag I had thrown in there. I dropped them at his feet and couldn't help but laugh as a little (I guess) chicken juice splashed him.

"Is this entirely necessary?" he asked.

"Yes."

"Honestly, it's fine if you don't want to tell me..."

"Shut up and give me a hand."

We both reached into the dumpster and pulled out the heavy black bag, carefully placing it on the floor.

"What is it?"

"It's a fucking bag, what do you think it is? Open it."

III

He wasn't going to let me not open it. Not after dragging me out here and fishing it out of the bin. I was nervous. I guess because I already knew what was in there. He'd whispered it enough to me during times when he thought I was asleep. He told me of the things he yearned to do. My hand was shaking like a leaf as I tugged at the knot.

"Hurry up," he rushed me.

"Just...Shut up!" I hissed back at him. I didn't need him getting in my face right about now. I didn't need him pressuring me into this. More to the point - I just didn't want to hear his voice right now as I continued to struggle with the knot. I just wanted silence. I needed silence. Needed to mentally prepare myself for what I was going to find.

The knot came apart in my shaking hands. This is it. Slowly, I pulled the two parts of bag away from each other and peered in. The contents were hard to see, not helped by the fact that the moon was hidden behind a multitude of clouds. Didn't keep the smell away from me though and I couldn't help but gag.

"What is it?" I asked, scared of the answer.

"Put your hand in."

"I don't want to."

"Put your fucking hand in. You wanted to know what I do. This is what I do."

I slowly put my hand in the bag and fumbled around. I felt something. What is that? Hair? Hair. I moved my hand further into the bag. Skin? Wet. What is this? I pulled my hand out of the bag and stood away from it.

"What the hell is this?" I asked. "What the hell is in that bag? What have you done?"

"So many questions, so many questions. Where would you like me to start?"

"What have you done?"

"A wasted question - you know what I've done."

"I need you to say it."

"I killed him."

"Who?"

"The boy."

"Stop fucking about with me!" I shouted. "What boy?!"

"Ooh - raising your voice at me, I'm impressed."

"I swear to God..."

"Shut up! This macho bullshit - it's not you. It doesn't suit you. You're just coming across as desperate."

"Desperate?! I am desperate! I'm desperate to know what you've done and why!"

"Tie the bag up and put it back in the dumpster. The sun will be up soon and we really don't want to get caught standing here. I promise that once you've done that you can go back to being macho and the big man...But for now - think with your fucking head."

"Put it back in the dumpster? You want it back in the bin? You put it back in the fucking bin!"

I turned away from him. I was done being his pawn. And I refused to tidy up what he had done. I wanted no part of it. I sat there - pissed - and watched as he lifted the bag back into the dumpster. Once again, just as he had done before, he buried it under the other bags we'd taken out. He slammed the lid down and walked back to the van. He jumped in the driver's seat. Guess I'm the passenger then. The van coughed into life as he turned the key in the ignition.

"What boy?" I asked him as he reversed us out of the alley. We hit the main road and he slammed the van into first gear before heading off in the direction we'd previously come from.

"The one from the park. The one who was crying constantly. His mum was shouting at him. She stormed off saying she'd go home without him. A common ploy put into play by desperate mothers. They think their threat of leaving without their child is supposed to scare them into running after them. Might work in some cases, but not in this instance. Mummy might have come back for him but it was too late. He wasn't there.."

"You snatched a child from the park? What if someone saw you...Where the fuck was I?"

"I don't know where you were. For all I know you stropped off because your day wasn't going as you'd hope it would. Quite frankly, I didn't give a fuck. I wanted to have some fun. I think I deserve that much..."

"By snatching a child from the park? Again - what if someone saw you? You put him in my fucking van."

"Where else was I going to put him?"

"Did someone see you? Oh shit, I don't even want to know."

"What the fuck do you take me for? No one saw me."

"We're going to jail. You know that, right?"

He didn't say anything. He just frowned as though his mind was going elsewhere. I don't even want to know where it went. If he was capable of...What...He killed a boy? If he could think of that - what the fuck else could he do? Don't question it. I don't want to know.

"We needed to do this," he said finally, breaking the silence between us.

"I'm a children's entertainer - why the fuck would I want to hurt a child?"

"It wasn't one of your children - one of your precious little darlings who enjoys laughing at your pathetic bullshit." His voice irritated me. It sounded like he was taunting me, trying to get a reaction from me, but what sort of reaction was I supposed to give after seeing what he had just done to a child? "The child was a cunt..."

"The child was just that...A child."

"A noisy, spoilt little shit cunt."

"Someone's son."

"Demon Seed."

"What the fuck is wrong with you?"

"Me? What's wrong with you? Hiding behind your day job. What happened tonight, what happened with the child - that is who we are. That is what we're about."

"No it isn't."

"Yes it is and the sooner you realise that - the better."

"Just don't even talk to me. I need to think about what we're going to do."

"What we're going to do? There's nothing to do."

"You think hiding a body in a dumpster is enough to keep us safe? You think they won't be able to trace the murder back to you? Back to us? And you say I'm an idiot? Jesus fucking Christ..."

"You need to calm down. You'll give yourself a brain aneurysm."

"Just - please - shut the fuck up."

"By morning, when you have had time to think about this properly, you'll come crawling to me. You'll realise this was the right thing to do. Is the right thing to do. So I killed an unhappy child. Big deal. They deserved it and - you know - they're probably up there in some fucking Heaven thanking me for what I did to them. Clearly they weren't happy with their mummy and daddy. I did them a favour..."

"SHUT UP!" I screamed at him. He stared at me via the rear-view mirror. There was an anger in his eyes I'd seen on more than one occasion. I shifted in my seat. I don't want to annoy him, not knowing what he was capable of, but I can't hear his voice right now. The man is poison. Pure poison. Sure - at times children could be irritating when they weren't happy but only because it's hard to get them to change their attitude when they're having a sulk. People like me, I just want to make the world smile. Children like that? If they were having a sulk about whatever - children like that are hard to make smile. It doesn't mean I'd want them to die. Especially at the hands of a psychopath.

We drove the remainder of the journey in silence. My mind focused on whether we were going to be caught for his crimes. My mind wondered whether there was a way out of it for me. Not him. He can go down for the crime. He deserves it. I don't though. This was all him. It was nothing to do with me. I'm fuming that he could even bring me into it without first checking with me. I angled myself in my seat so I could see him in the side mirror of the van; he looked like he was as fuming as I was. Well stuff him. I don't owe him anything. I'll wait until morning and then I'll turn him in. The authorities might go easy on me if I turn him in. It would go a long way to show I'm not a part of what he did. It was all him.

I don't owe him anything.

5.

I hadn't slept all night. I had lain awake, tossing and turning. Occasionally, I heard him trying to talk to me - trying to say something - but I ignored him. Whatever he had to say, I didn't want to hear it. My mind was too caught up with getting taken in by the police when the crime is discovered.

The sun shone through the cracks in the curtains reminding me that it was a new day. All night I had been wrestling with what would be the best course of action in my mind and - only now - had I finally come to a decision. The thought I had whilst he drove us home was the best way to go. For me at least. Phone the police.

I rolled off the bed and reached across to where my mobile phone was charging on the bedside cabinet. I unlocked the touch-screen and went through to the keypad function. I pressed the first nine. My finger wavered over the nine when I heard him speak to me.

"What are you fucking doing?"

"What I have to do."

"Jesus. Have you heard yourself? You think you're so fucking high and mighty. Well - fine - phone them then, if that's what you think is the right thing to do."

"Of course it is. You're a murderer!"

"So are you. Your prints are on his face just as mine are."

"I'll tell them you took me there to show me what you did and that I reached into the bag because it was too dark to see. That's the truth."

He laughed, "And you think they'll believe you? You're even more fucking pathetic than I first thought."

"Me? I'm not the one killing children."

"Call them then. They'll take us both down but if that's what you want to do, I won't stand in your way. Here, fuck it, I'll even help." He called my bluff by pressing the second nine. "Come on, just one more press and both of our lives are over."

"Only yours."

"You're sure about that? They'll somehow take me away and leave you behind? The innocent party in all of this?"

"I am innocent."

"From where I stand, you have as much blood on your hands as I do. Anyway - sorry - I didn't mean to distract you. I believe you were in the middle of making a phone call? Please. Don't let me stop you."

"Fuck you!" I threw the phone onto the bed.

"No balls. You lack conviction in everything you do."

"Don't push me," I hissed.

"Why ever not? The worst you're going to do is shout and whinge at me. Although, to be fair, that is irritating. Gives me a headache whenever you talk..."

"You give me a headache."

"Well isn't this the most childish of conversations! You spend too much time with kiddies. Surprised you're not dating one of them."

"Fuck off."

"Unless that's why you're upset I killed the boy? You think it's a waste of prime meat? Maybe next time I should have given you some alone time first...You know - let you fuck the virgin ass before I stuck a knife through his eye."

"Is that how you did it?" His words made me feel cold to the core.

"Fuck his ass?"

"Stuck a knife through his eye."

"You want the details?"

I hesitated. I wasn't sure if I wanted them or not. I wasn't sure if I wanted to hear how he killed an innocent child. Part of me wanted to know (I guess that much was obvious) and part of me wanted to bury any knowledge of what he'd done. I felt a sickness brewing within the pit of my stomach.

"You're not going to be sick, are you?" he asked. "Maybe you want a little time in the bathroom first?"

"Just tell me. What did you do?"

"You going to tell the police?"

"I'm not sure."

"Because if you are, I'd rather you just listened in on the conversation with them. Not sure I want to be repeating myself all day long, you know?"

"Just tell me!" I shouted. My voice echoed through the room.

He sat on the edge of the bed and picked the phone up before clearing the screen from the previous dialled numbers. He set the phone to one side, back on the bedside cabinet. He hesitated a moment as he cast his mind back to the previous day.

"Like I said," he started, "you disappeared - not sure where. I figured you were just in a mood because your day hadn't gone as you planned. You know, what with the cancelled party and then the poor reaction in the park...So I was waiting by the van so I could catch a lift home and I heard all this commotion. This woman was screaming at her child for some reason or other. She ended up getting in her car and wheel-spinning from the car park as though abandoning him there. He didn't seem to care. Just stood there screaming his head off, you know - a proper fucking rant. God only knows what it was about. It was embarrassing."

"Children play up from time to time."

"Yes - and should be shot for it. You want me to fucking finish?" I didn't say anything. I waited patiently for him to continue his story. He took another deep breath and continued, "So this bastard thing was screaming and screaming. I looked around and the mother wasn't coming back. Fuck knows where she had disappeared too, and there wasn't anyone else coming to his aid. No one else was even around, to be honest. Seems most of the park was empty at that time but then - you did decide to leave it really late. Why was that?"

"I was touting for business."

"You sure about that? Or were you waiting for the perfect opportunity to snatch a child?"

I ignored him. I knew what he was trying to do. He was trying to bait me into an argument with him. He was trying to get me to say what he did was right, the decent thing to do. But I wouldn't admit it. I'd never admit it. You can't go around killing children. It wasn't right. Murder is bad but it's worse when children are involved. I tried to get him to continue the story, "So you snatched him?"

He nodded, "Threw him in the back of your van."

"How did I not hear him?"

"That would be the punch to his head. Knocked him clean out. I tell you what, too, the blissful silence of the day when he stopped screaming. Heaven."

"You're sick."

"Because I like peace and quiet? Whatever."

"The mum - she would have come back."

"She did come back."

"What?!"

"Asked me if I'd seen her son. I asked her if she meant the one who was screaming in the middle of the car park and she just looked embarrassed. Can you imagine that? Embarrassed by your own child. I wonder how many parents feel like that? You make them - you should stand by them no matter what; whether they're making a scene in the car park or whether you find them a weak disappointment of a child...You should stand by them. The fact she didn't - clearly she didn't want him..."

"Or she was trying to..."

"Don't try and justify it. You weren't there."

"What did she say?" I changed the subject back to the story to save another argument.

"When I told her I had seen him, she asked where he went. Of course I pointed her out in a completely different direction. Said he headed to the park."

"She believed you?"

He shrugged. "I even offered to help her find him. Because that's the nice sort of fella that I am."

"You're sick." I wanted to grab for the mobile phone but knew I wouldn't be able to phone the police, no matter how much I wanted to. He'd always stop me. "When did you kill him?" I asked.

"I brought us home. Couldn't very well kill him in the van, could I?"

"Where did you do it?"

"It's not important."

"It is to me..."

My mobile phone started to buzz on the bedside cabinet signifying an incoming call. With each buzz it danced a little further across the wooden top. I looked in its direction.

"You going to get that?" he asked.

I wanted to but, at the same time, I didn't want to stop this conversation. I wanted to know all the details. For some reason I thought it might have made me feel a little better to know what had happened. That, maybe, I'd be able to come to terms with it. Was that even possible? A child had died because of us. Was there any coming back from that or had we crossed a line which could never be taken back?

Without any warning he reached across to the phone and took a hold of it. He accepted the call and pressed the phone to my ear. Didn't really give me much of a choice but to talk to the person on the other end of it.

"Hello?" I asked, trying my best to sound normal. Trying my best to sound as though I wasn't in the middle of a discussion detailing how a child had died the night before. Does guilt even come across in the tone of someone's voice?

I listened to the man (Mr. Cartwright) introduce himself on the other end of the telephone. He explained that he'd seen me at a party a couple of weeks ago and his own son's birthday was fast approaching. Apparently, his son couldn't stop talking about me since he'd seen me and so Mr. Cartwright wanted to hire me. I felt my mind screaming at me not to accept the booking. I heard the voices say I should just hang the phone up and then other voices say I should go; if I suddenly disappeared now, without word, it would just look more suspicious. Mr. Cartwright was unaware of my internal debating and proceeded to ask me for my rates.

He answered for me. I wanted to scream at him to shut the fuck up but I knew Mr. Cartwright would hear and - more importantly - that he wouldn't understand. Before I knew it, he had gone one step further to accept the booking. I wanted to ask him what he was playing at but - again - I knew I couldn't. I could only sit there as he reached for the diary which was always kept close to my mobile phone. This coming Saturday was clear until he started to pencil in Mr. Cartwright's address. Please stop. Tell him we're busy. Tell him we have a booking. He doesn't need to know we're not accepting them at the moment because we killed someone last night. He doesn't need to know any of that. Just that we're busy. Tell him.

My heart sank as Mr. Cartwright thanked me for my time. He responded on my behalf once again before putting the phone down. He threw it to one side, with the diary, and lay back on the bed with a self-satisfied smug look on his face.

"We make quite the team," he said.

"We can't go to that booking. You need to call him back," I said.

"Forgot to get his number. Sorry. This is why you take your own bookings. I've never been one for this side of the business."

"This side of the business? What other sides are there?"

"We provide a service. That's what I wanted to show you last night."

"What are you talking about?"

"You entertain the good children. I punish the bad. It's quite simple."

My heart skipped a beat.

"You can't do that again," I hissed. "What you did last night - that was it - you can't do it anymore."

He smiled, "If you watched the news - you'd know I can do it again. And I have done it again..."

"What? What are you talking about?" Had he killed more than one child? If so, how many? What were the numbers and where was I when he was doing it? The sickness brewed within my twisting gut once more. He didn't answer me though. I screamed at him to tell me what he meant. I screamed at him to answer my questions but he didn't. He just sat there, smiling. And then, without a word, he disappeared from my sight. "Talk to me!" I screamed at him but he was gone. I jumped up from the bed and ran through to the landing. I called out for him to come back and talk but he ignored me. I screamed and dropped to my knees, surprised tears streaming down my face as I felt both the weight of what he'd just told me and the weight of what we'd been a part of the previous night.

II

I was going from room to room. I was out of breath, I was moving so fast. Not sure exactly what I was looking for. Just something, I guess, to let me know whether he'd brought the boy into the house. After all if he didn't do it here, where else would he have done it? There was nowhere else I knew of which would have given him the privacy to carry out such an atrocity.

At first I thought he'd done it in the van but the rear was completely clear of any evidence and yet was still messy from where I hadn't cleaned it for ages. Impossible to clean up the evidence without showing some trace that a cleaning operation had recently taken place.

In the house I had a good look around the living room and nothing was out of place. At least, nothing which hadn't been left out of place by myself. The study - a small room - was seemingly undisturbed too; the layers of dust again suggesting no clean up had taken place. The room was dusty as I rarely went in there. Only went in once every couple of months to try and get a head start on my accounts and, during those times, I never thought to give it a clean. Upstairs only had a modest sized bathroom and a couple of bedrooms and those too looked as though they hadn't played a part in what he had done.

The final room to check was the kitchen. I walked in, wondering why I hadn't checked here first. After all, this was the room I had seen him in that night, acting suspiciously. I cast my mind back to what he was doing - ah yes, the washing machine. I opened the door and pulled my work uniform out. I gave it a shake and examined it. Seemed to be okay. He wouldn't have worn this anyway, would he? He hates me wearing it. Unless he'd put it on that night in order to frame me should he have been discovered? Would he have done that? I wasn't sure but I couldn't put it past him. It's not as though the two of us are close.

I dropped the uniform in a crumpled pile by my feet and continued to scan the room for evidence of foul play. Nothing. The place was spotless. Well - as spotless as things got in my house. I froze. My eyes were fixed upon a door in the corner of the room. One which I tended to keep shut. To people visiting, they'd have presumed it led to nothing but a cupboard but that wasn't the case; it was the door to what was originally intended, I presume, to be a wine cellar. I had never used it. Only been down there once and that was when I first moved in and I was exploring the home. There was something about the room - some energy - something down there...It made me feel uncomfortable. I got out of there as fast as I could and I vowed never to go back down there. Soon, I didn't even see the door when I went into the kitchen. I was blind to it. With this feeling running through the pit of my stomach, I wished I was still blind to it. I can't be though. I need to go down there. I need to see. Already know what's down there...Need to go down. Shit.

I walked across the kitchen floor and reached out for the handle. What are the chances of getting down there without him knowing? Does it even matter if he finds me, or knows I've been down there? I reached out and took a hold of the handle. I paused a moment, unsure as to whether he was going to come running in to try and stop me from seeing anything I shouldn't have. Nothing. Silence in fact. I paused a moment longer; not to give him further chance, but to enjoy the silence. It had been too long since I'd had pure silence in my life. It's blissful. A child screaming in the back of my mind snapped me back to reality. What? I'm supposed to hear the child screaming now too as though I'd been present for his murder?! I wasn't there. It was nothing to do with me. Fucking guilt consuming me.

For my own peace of mind, I turned the door handle and leaned into the cellar. Hanging by the side of the wall, before the first of twelve steps down, was a piece of string connected to the light-switch. I gave it a tug, half-expecting the bulb to be dead. It slowly flickered into life, illuminating the room below me. Shadows cast from the overhanging light revealed the room wasn't empty. Proof he had been down there. I remember the room as being empty.

III

"Where do you think you're going?" I hissed in his ear as I stopped him from venturing further down the stairs.

"Get out of my way."

"You have no business down there."

"It's my house. I can go where I want."

"You never wanted this room. You left it for me. You have no right..."

"I never said I didn't want this room!"

"You're scared to be in here. Because you're a fucking pussy."

"I'm going down there."

"You're not."

IV

I pushed past him and made my way down the stairs, each step creaking underneath my weight. My mouth fell upon when I reached the bottom step and saw into the cellar.

"What the fuck is this?" I asked.

He didn't need to answer. It was obvious as to what it was. The question I should have asked was what the hell was all of this doing in the cellar.

"What does it fucking look like?" he hissed.

"It looks like you've been hiding a lot from me."

I stepped off the last of the steps, onto the cold concrete of the cellar floor - unsure of where to look first, my mind temporarily distracted from the real reason I was down here.

6.

There were different shaped easels set up around the room. Canvases were perched on top of them - some blank and some already stained with oil paint. The floor was littered with painting instruments, different sized brushes thrown here and there with no rhyme nor reason. He's been coming down painting? What the hell? I understood why he kept what he did with the child a secret from me but why hide this? If anything, this was the sort of thing we should have been sharing...I froze on the spot as my eyes fixed upon a pile of canvases leaning against the wall. Considering the front canvas is finished - I'm guessing all of these have been completed. I just hoped that they didn't all have the same picture painted upon them - more specifically the same subject matter. I walked over to the pile and lifted the front one up to get a closer look.

"A work of art, don't you think?" he whispered in my ear.

The picture was a close-up portrait of a small boy from the torso upwards. He was naked. His eyes stared out of the painting. It didn't matter which way I tilted the picture, they seemed to stay fixed on me. A haunting, dead expression. The boy's mouth was slightly agape, his tongue visibly lulling to one side There was a wide cut across his throat and you could clearly see the inner workings of his throat through the rip. Was this real? A portrait of the boy he killed? I didn't see his face when I felt into the bag. I just touched his face. I don't know what he looked like. This could be him. Is it?

"Who is this?" I needed to know.

He smiled, "You know who."

"The child you took me to?"

He nodded.

"You killed him and painted him?"

He nodded again.

That could only mean that…I lowered the picture and noticed, for the first time, a small bed in the corner of the room. Chains either end of it. A mattress stained with red, brown and yellow. I gagged. So they lie there, dead, and he stands here watching over them, painting them as though no crime has been committed? I looked down at the pictures. The second one was of a different figure. What were the chances he just had a good imagination and it was the same dead child but with a different face painted? I looked to him. He was standing there, shaking his head as though he knew what I was thinking.

"They're all dead?" I asked.

He nodded. I gagged again as I suppressed the need to vomit. How long had he been doing this, killing innocent children? How hadn't he been stopped already? I wanted to tear him apart limb from limb but I knew I couldn't. I looked down at the pictures and reached for another, throwing the one of the boy with the slit throat to one side.

"Be careful with that. Might be worth something one day," he said.

I pulled a second painting out from the middle of the pile and was immediately horrified: the image of what appeared to be a young girl's body. Her legs had been cut off at the top of her thigh, her arms cut off from the elbows and her head cut off at the neck. All pieces which had been removed were missing from the picture. It was literally just her torso. Where the limbs had been removed there were harsh red brushstrokes, with a similar brushstroke over where her genitals would have been.

"A personal favourite," he said, glee in his voice.

I threw the picture across the room as I reached for another. I could hear him huffing and puffing at me – irritated, no doubt, by my lack of care. Well sorry, but I didn't care. If I could have, I would have thrown him across the room. A third picture was primarily of an eyeball. It was balanced in a hand and sliced down the middle. In the background of the painting was what appeared to be a young boy crying. He was huddled up into a ball, a harsh red brushstroke coming from a black hole where his left eye should have been.

"How his screaming didn't wake you up, I don't know."

I dropped the picture and looked at the remaining pile. I had seen enough of them, but was giving them a quick count where they rested on the floor. Over twenty of them.

"They're all finished paintings?" I asked.

He nodded.

We both just stood there a moment. I didn't have a clue as to what to say. I think, going by the buzz in my head, he had plenty to say but was giving me the time needed to process it. Well, silly really, there wasn't enough time in the world to process what he'd shown me already and now this on top of that? I could never understand what would drive a person to do such a thing.

I lunged forward and knocked one of the easels over. A second later and I knocked over the second and third until they were all on the floor. He didn't say anything. He just watched. I guess he knew I needed to vent my initial feelings of anger from my body or else there'd never be any hope of us moving on from this. Moving on from this? Why am I thinking like that? There's no way we can move on from this. As far as I am concerned, we're done.

I gave a final look around the room and hurried up the stairs before I accidentally saw something else which I wouldn't like. Can't take anymore. Back in the kitchen, I slammed the door shut before struggling to move the kitchen table across the floor in an effort to block it. That door never needs to be opened again. He still remained silent. He just stood there, watching what I was doing. With the table in place, I dropped to my knees and started to weep for the children.

II

I'm loath to call it a make-up table because it sounds so feminine but I guess that's what it is. A table, against my bedroom wall, a few feet away from my bed, with a small oval shaped mirror. It may look strange to people looking in, a single man of my age with a set up like this. I suppose, thinking into it a little more, it could be perceived that I'm a widower with the table and mirror - the whole set-up - belonging to my dead partner. Not the case though. There is a perfectly valid reason as to why it is here though, and that's because I need to apply my 'work' make-up somewhere. Sure, I could do it in the bathroom but it's easier to put it on whilst sitting comfortably.

I was sitting at the table now. My eyes were red raw from crying. My skin was so pale. I haven't looked as though I'm in the best shape for as long as I can remember but - even so - I feel as though I've aged dramatically over the weekend.

I had all my work get-up out, spread across the table: a children's face-painting set. I could have bought professional make-up to get the look but I found this to be more than adequate. It also happened to be a lot cheaper.

"You can't ignore what you've seen."

I took the lid off the white colour and dipped the sponge into it. I looked into the mirror one last time before applying make-up and smiled. The first time I'd seen this particular face and smiled. I'm not smiling because I am happy with it. I'm smiling at it because it's soon to disappear.

"I'll still be here."

I pressed the sponge onto my forehead and wiped over my brow. Every piece of visible skin (neck, face, ears) was to be coloured in this pasty white colour; a good foundation for the other colours needed - such as the purple rings around the eyes and the overly large smile drawn on.

"You can't bury me."

The whole face takes approximately ten to twenty minutes to complete, closer to the latter if I want it to look really professional. Right now, I'm not too worried. I just want to hide him from my sight. Help silence him.

"You're being a fucking retard!"

III

I was standing in front of the full-size mirror I had stashed in the second bedroom. I was in my full get-up. The face was finished; I'd put the yellow wig on this time around and slid into the red jump-suit - my oldest one and - to look at it - you could tell. Definitely seen better days and, truth be told, I should have potentially thrown it out a long time ago. Not sure why I haven't; a difficulty in letting go of the past? Not sure why that is - wasn't exactly the best. Despite not planning to leave the house I had also stepped into the large clown shoes. Also red. I smiled as broadly as I could - accentuated by the use of the make-up. Not sure if I actually look very kiddy-friendly today or whether I look sinister.

I waved at myself, a gentle side by side with my hand.

Definitely sinister.

Was that how I always looked? Had I just not noticed it before? Or is this just because of him? He has tainted how I feel about myself in either guise. I'm not sure. Hopefully I've always looked like this - rather that than know he has managed to change me within the space of a night. Maybe it's the smile? Maybe I need to tone it down a little bit? I changed the smile to a less dramatic one. I still feel as though I look evil.

Please let me have always looked like this. Please. Please let it be that I'm just feeling paranoid about it now he's made me part of his little hobby. Please. Don't let him have changed me.

"I haven't changed you," he hissed in my ear, "you're the one who changed. If anyone changed anyone, it was you changing me."

I saw him in the mirror's reflection. He looked expressionless as he stared back at me with cold, dead eyes. I flinched and lashed forward with my right fist, smashing the mirror in the process.

He laughed, "Whoops. That's seven years bad luck for you then."

IV

I was sitting in front of the television (in full make-up) with the volume turned as loud as it could go in an effort to drown out his grating voice. One of my DVDs was playing on the screen in an effort to bury the horrors I had discovered over the last few hours, not that the film was doing a very good job of it. In the background of every scene, I couldn't help but see the images of dead children mingling with the other onscreen extras as though they'd always been there, part of the film, and I was only just seeing it. At one point - twenty minutes into the film - I momentarily believed they had always been there and that he had simply opened my eyes to it.

They couldn't have been real, the pictures in the basement. Surely. They couldn't have been real pictures of real people he had killed. They couldn't have been. A mumbled, distorted voice told me they were real but I ignored it. They were most likely fake pictures. Scenarios he imagined in his troubled mind. Yes, that was it. They were the work of a sick individual and not the product of a genuine crime. There's a big market for sick and disturbing images like that - clearly he is just trying to tap into it a little? Maybe, if I were to look around on auction sites on the Internet, I'd find links to where they're being sold? Of course. All makes sense when you think about it. A mumbled voice asked me about the body I saw.

"I didn't see the body," I said, despite meaning to ignore him. "For all I know, you're just messing with me. You're trying to make me think we killed someone. That's all. A sick game to try and mess with my head. Although I don't understand why."

The voice mumbled something under the shouting of the film playing on the screen. I reached for the controller and killed the volume in the hope he would admit the truth to me; it was just a sick prank to try and teach me some kind of lesson, whatever that could be.

"What about the bed in the corner of the room? The stained mattress?" he asked.

Maybe that was there from a previous occupant and he'd just left it there as moving it was too much hassle. That would make sense. It's not as though I go into the room so he knew I probably wouldn't have helped him dispose of it.

"If you're that sure it is all a prank, you'll be happy to watch the news," he sneered. "Look at the time. It's coming up to twelve now, the lunchtime bulletins." He showed me his watch and it was indeed coming up to the lunchtime news program. "If you're that sure it's a prank, change the channel."

"I can't," I told him, "and you know I can't. It's an old set. Won't receive digital transmissions."

He laughed.

"What's so funny?"

"The television accepts digital transmissions. What do you think that box is?" He pointed down to a small black box which sat next to the DVD unit. I'd never noticed it before. How long had it been there? "Television just needed an upgrade and that was easy enough to sort." He picked the television controller up and switched the channel.

Adverts came onto screen, the first time I had seen any for as long as I could remember.

"You never told me."

"You never seemed bothered. Every time you watched the television it was always one of your silly films."

"They're not silly."

"Whatever." He pointed to the screen, "Here you go."

The news' opening credits rang through the living room. The programme opened with a story about a children's entertainer who'd been arrested after a number of people stepped forward to make child molestation accusations against him, dating back thirty years.

"There's some sick people out there," he whispered.

There was a second story about some affairs happening overseas. I didn't listen to what was said as I knew it was most likely to be scaremongering. Most stories about foreign affairs seemed to be designed just for that - a way of making us feel at ease about the government's latest plan to push forward with stepping in and getting involved. Why they couldn't just keep their noses out of business which didn't directly concern them I do not know. It's not as though they need to...I stopped mid-thought. My eyes were transfixed to the screen: a picture of a smiling child that had been taken on a bright, sunny day in what appeared to be a back garden. He was sitting on a swing, a padding pool to the side of the photo and fences behind him.

"He didn't look like that at the park," he said.

"Shut up!" I hissed.

The story ran through. The boy had disappeared from the park yesterday afternoon. Jack, aged nine. His parents were said to be distraught. Any information and you were invited to phone through, with a number provided.

"You really did it?"

He nodded, "I did say so."

"The pictures are all real?"

"Good, aren't they?"

"They're not just what you imagined?"

"No. They're real. Just as I told you." He hesitated, "So what do you think? It feels right, doesn't it?"

"What are you talking about? They're fucking looking for him!"

"They're not looking for him. Relax."

"Did you not just watch that?! His picture was on the news. It's probably in the papers too. They want their son back!" I shouted.

"Calm down!" he shouted back. He waited until I was calmer before continuing, "They're not looking for him. They don't give a shit about him. And I can't say I blame them - the whiney little cunt."

"He was on the news."

"A picture which did not represent the boy I took was on the news. People will be looking for the kid shown in the pictures, not the one I disposed of."

"Are you fucking insane? They're the same person."

"Are they? Are they really?" He stood up and walked us through to the bathroom. He looked into the mirror. "What do you see?" He was staring at me, his eyes almost rabid with excitement. He screamed at me, "What do you fucking see?!"

"I see you."

"And I see you. Are we not one and the same?"

"I am nothing like you."

"You are me!"

"I'm not!"

"When people see me, they see you."

"No. When people see you, they see a monster. When they see me, they see an entertainer."

"Then - by your own argument - the boy in the picture is not the same as the boy I took…They are two different people and if that's the case…They will never find him." I stormed from the bathroom and slammed the door shut. "Admit it - we got away with it. Just as we always get away with it."

"Why can't you leave me alone?" I begged him. I hurried through back to the living room and slammed that door shut too. I just wanted some peace and quiet. I sat myself down on the sofa and flicked the television channel back over to Laurel and Hardy.

"Why do you keep denying who you really are?" he whispered in my ear. He didn't sound annoyed, as he had done so before. In fact, if anything, this was the kindest I had ever heard his voice. Almost compassionate. Had it been the first time I'd ever spoken to him, I may have believed him to be sincere. But it wasn't the first time I'd met him. And I knew who he really was. A murderer. "You could be so much happier if you just stopped lying to yourself…" I reached for the controller and went to turn the television back up to its maximum level. "You want space?" he asked. "Fine. But just so you know, I'm going out tonight and I'd very much like for you to join me."

"Where are you going?"

"If you want to know - you'll come with me," he said with a broad smile on his face. "You know where to find me."

7.

The rest of the day was filled with thoughts of the dead children. I couldn't help but picture how frantic their parents must have been, desperate for their safe return. He seemed to relish the pain he caused the children, the fact he killed them. He couldn't seem to understand that they were someone's child. Someone out there loved them no matter what he thought of them, whether they were being too loud with their screaming or tantrums or whatever. He didn't have the right to end their lives. No one had the right to do so.

In the brief moments where I wasn't thinking about the dead, I found myself growing concerned about what he had planned for the night. Maybe I should go with him? Perhaps, if I did so, I could stop him from doing whatever he wanted to do. But then what if I couldn't stop him? What if I had to witness it first hand? The atrocious acts he was capable of carrying out sickened me, yes, but they also frightened the hell out of me. It's one thing to see painted pictures of what he once did but it's another thing altogether to witness the act itself. It didn't matter how many times he tried to tell me I needed to join him, I needed to be a part of it - I didn't want to. I couldn't see it. I couldn't be a part of it.

When I went upstairs, I carefully moved all of the furniture against the bedroom door. I wasn't being careful so as not to damage it though. I was being careful so as not to disturb him. Had he caught me moving the bits and pieces, he would have easily stopped me - far more easily than I could have stopped him when it came to carrying out his heinous acts anyway.

I knew the blockade wouldn't stop him but I hoped, regardless, that it would at least put him off from trying to go out. Perhaps a laziness stopping him from bothering to start moving things back to where they belonged? I hoped so.

I sat on the edge of the bed and stared ahead at the blockade, unblinking. It was getting late now and I knew it would only be a matter of time before he sees what I've done. May as well use the last bit of quiet time to mentally prepare myself for an argument. I kept asking myself why I was putting myself through this and delaying the inevitable. The man was sick. He didn't need locking in his bedroom like a reprimanded teenager, he needed proper psychiatric help; help that I was unable to offer him even if he were prepared to listen. I should just phone the police. I should just warn them of him and let them deal with him, whether that be putting him in jail or a mental health facility; he needed to be removed from the streets before he hurt anyone else. But where would that leave me? We weren't the same person. I didn't deserve the same treatment and yet that's exactly what I would get. They'd tar me with the same brush. Not just the authorities but everyone else too; all those who'd get to learn of what he did to those poor children. Even if they'd go easy on me - the courts and professionals - the stigma the crimes would carry with them...That's the sort of thing that would never leave you.

I reached down to the small make-up mirror on the floor and picked it up. It had toppled off from the table when I was dragging the whole thing across to the doorway. I hadn't bothered to pick it up as the additional weight wouldn't have done anything to help with the blockade. I looked at my reflection in the shattered mirror. Due to the various cracks, there were lots of my made-up face looking back at myself. I couldn't help but wonder which was the real one. So many faces, so many potential personalities. Was there a 'real one' or were they all necessary to form the bigger picture? I threw the mirror back to the floor and was relieved when it broke a little more until it was at the point of now being completely useless to use. I wished I could curl up into a little ball and just wither away into nothing. More than that, I wished I'd not been born at all as thoughts turned to my mother and father.

They divorced when I was young. Mother moved away and I found myself left with my father, a stern man who liked a drink. His demons mostly came at night where he then found the need to take them out on me. By morning, he'd always come into my cramped bedroom apologising and hungover, but I could never trust him. Even when he promised me it would never happen again, I could never take him at his word. There was always a part of me which waited for the night-time monster to come crawling into the bedroom - that look on his face. I shook the image from my mind. I don't need to be thinking about that now - not whilst I am feeling vulnerable.

I lay back on the bed and shut my eyes. The blackness provided by my closed eyelids was nice. It made me feel at peace with the world, despite knowing there was no such joy to be experienced. I wished it could last forever. Who knows, with a little encouragement like - say - the tip of a blade against my wrist, maybe it could?

II

I woke with a jump to the sound of his irate voice. I must have fallen asleep. Hardly surprising, considering the fact it's quite late now and I hadn't slept much the previous night when we got home, despite feeling as though I were absolutely shattered. He was standing up and staring at the blockade I had prepared for him in front of the bedroom doorway.

"What is this? This some kind of fucking joke?"

"No joke."

"This is supposed to stop me how exactly? I'll just move it."

"Look - whatever you're planning tonight - just stay in. Stay in with me and we can talk."

"Talk? You're having a fucking joke. Very good. Funny. Nearly had me there.

Come on - give me a hand moving this shit out of the way. I have things to do, places to be..."

"I'm not moving anything. I mean it. Don't go out. Stay home. Talk to me. We need to know what we're going to do from here on in."

"What the fuck are you talking about? Seriously? I know what I'm going to do. I'm going to go to a bar and I'm going to get some fucking drinks inside of me and see where the night takes me. You're more than welcome to join me. Who knows - maybe we can pick up some skank and have ourselves a little three-way. In fact, fuck it, you want to bond? That's what we'll do. We'll have ourselves a three-way. See if we can meet in the middle. What say you?"

"No."

"No?"

"No."

"No. What? That's it? Just no."

"I'm not going out with you. I don't want you to go out. I want us to stay in and talk things through like adults."

"Adults? You're dressed as a fucking clown and you want to talk things through like adults? Fuck, man, you should be a standup comic. You're coming out with some funny shit tonight." His voice changed and became even more hostile in what seemed to be a blink of an eye, "Now help me move this fucking shit out of my fucking way before I do you some fucking damage. Understand?"

I sat on the bed. He can threaten me all he likes but I won't help him. I want no part in this. Just as I want no part in going out with him to try and bond over the back of some drunken whore.

He waited for me to help and then realised I wasn't going to, "Fine. Fuck you too."

He hopped to the blockade and started throwing the items across the room in an effort to get out.

III

He's a fucking child if he thinks this is going to stop me. What? A few bits of furniture thrown in front of the fucking door and - bam - just like that he thinks he has me trapped? Absolutely pathetic. I grabbed his precious make-up table and lifted it clean off the floor.

"Please be careful with that."

"What? This?" I threw it across the room and watched with glee as it splintered into pieces over the bedroom floor. Had he really given a shit about it, he wouldn't have used it to try and block my path. He should expect everything in my way to get broken because I aim to smash it all. Teach him - maybe - that he has absolutely fuck all control over me. I heard him cry out when the table broke. A possible lesson learned. I picked up the next item in my way - the chair that went with the make-up table - and launched it at the window as hard as I could. It smashed through, sending glass flying to the floor outside.

"Okay. Wait. Let me get it for you."

"No - seriously - it's fine. You just fucking stand there and watch. I've got it."

I grabbed at the chest of drawers, the last item in my way, and toppled it over with a hard shove to the side. It crashed to the floor, sending the items within spilling out all over the place. At least we know what he'll be doing tomorrow whilst I'm getting over my hangover. He'll be cleaning. I reached forward and grabbed the door handle. I twisted it and pulled it open.

"Wait. Please. Come on. We need to talk."

I stood there in the doorway for a moment. I could stay and talk to him but what was the point? He'd only carry on with the same bullshit about how I am wrong for doing what I do. The same crap I'd heard time and time before. I wished I could believe him about wanting to actually talk. Not what he wanted to talk about but what we needed to talk about. I shook my head and headed off down the stairs. It won't be a discussion about what needs to be discussed. No sense wasting my time. At the bottom of the stairs, I threw my Chuck Taylors on, trying my best to keep my back to him to avoid anymore pathetic conversations. With my shoes on, I walked over to the front door and reached out for the handle. I paused. I'll give him one more chance. I slowly turned back to him.

"One more chance," I said.

"For what?"

"To come with me."

I could see he wanted to come. He was tempted. But it wasn't because of the reasons I wanted him to accompany me. I could see it was because he thought it gave him more chances to turn me away from the path I was set upon.

"Forget it," I told him. I reached over to the side where the keys to his van were hanging. "I'm borrowing your van," I said. I didn't wait for him to argue with me. I turned back to the front door and let myself out, slamming the door behind me.

I walked over to the van and climbed in. I slid the key into the ignition and leaned back, catching a sight of myself in the rear-view mirror. Fuck me. Still dressed like a fucking clown. That's just fucking brilliant. I put my hands on the steering wheel and screamed out in a blind fit of rage. That fucking cunt is starting to get to me. Well I can't go back in. I can't go and get changed - not with him in there. It will just invite the possibility of more conversation. Fuck it. It doesn't matter. At least if anyone sees me, they won't actually see the real me. They'll see him. I get to have the fun, he gets to take the fall. Sure I'll go down with him, but they'll know it was him. They might go easy on me. I fired the engine up and slammed the van into reverse. Sooner I get out of here, the better.

IV

I like these calmer moments. He isn't around. He isn't whining in my ear; pathetic little cunt that he is. It's peaceful. Even when I have company and they're screaming. To me - it's still a calm moment.

I don't have company with me tonight though, as I drive around in his holly-jolly fucking van. Shame there aren't any garages open where I can part exchange this heap of shit - not that people would be happy to take it off my hands. I'd probably end up owing them money.

With the house out of sight, in the rear-view mirror, I pulled the van over to the side of the road and reached across to the glove compartment where he stored his satellite navigation system. I pulled it out, along with the plug in cable, and plugged it into the cigarette lighter. The screen shone to life as I waited a few seconds for the menu screen to become available.

"Come on, come on," I said - could my words hurry it up? The menu screen appeared on the small display offering up various options. The one I wanted was the choice for 'most recent'. I pressed into it and selected the top postcode.

A message flashed up a second later, informing me it was calculating the route.

"Thank you, modern technology."

I never paid attention when he did the driving. If you told me I had to go to where he'd be only a couple of hours earlier, I would never have been able to get there. Not without stopping and asking for directions anyway. Thanks to wonderful tools such as this, all I had to do was press a few buttons. A couple of buttons and - just like that - I am guided there via the quickest possible route.

"Where possible, perform a u-turn," the machine ordered me.

I selected the first gear and did a clumsy three-point turn (actually a four-point turn) in the road before heading back in the direction I had just come from, a beaming smile on my face as I drove. He should have come with me tonight. He may be on the fence about what I do in my spare time but - I think - this could have changed his opinion. This could have made him see the light. Maybe I'll take a little project home. Keep it downstairs until he is ready to watch; ready to lend a helping hand so he can understand - and see - how much pleasure there is to be gained from it.

I drove for about twenty minutes or so, following the route offered to me via the satnav, and eventually pulled into the road I was looking for. He hadn't entered a house number when he'd previously put in the postcode for the property but that was fine - I didn't need an exact number. I wasn't good at remembering directions but I was when it came to remembering what the properties looked like. I drove to the end of the road, away from where I actually wanted to be, and let the van roll to a stop.

It has gone midnight now. All of the houses have their lights off with the exception of one at the far end of the street. Night owls I guess. Bad news for people like me as it increases the chance of someone seeing me - and it's hard enough to remain inconspicuous whilst driving around in this clapped out heap of shit.

I leaned to the key, sticking from the ignition, and turned it counter-clockwise, killing the engine in the process. As I sat back in my seat, pulling they key out in the process, I turned my attention to the house I had come to visit.

"Iron Man is cool," I mumbled, "even if it is a dodgy outfit. There's no escaping that." I hesitated a moment, "Why couldn't we dress up like Iron Man? Instead I get to be Bobo the fucking clown. So queer." I jumped out of the van and walked towards the house, avoiding the street lamps as I did so. The trick about doing this is to remain in the shadows as much as possible so there's less chance of detection. "Regardless of how we dress up though, that doesn't detract from the fact it's just fucking rude to cancel at the last minute - or, worse yet, pretend you've cancelled. What if we'd turned down other bookings just to attend this one? It doesn't matter what I think of the job; at the end of the day it is a job and it puts food in both of our mouths."

I pushed my way through the bush and stomped my way up the garden to the front door.

"If he apologises, I'll let him off."

I reached up with my gloved finger and pressed the doorbell.

"A sorry and - I don't know - half of the fee. Yes. That would go down very well."

V

As quickly as I could, I dragged him from the front porch and threw him into the bush before hiding myself. I put my hand over his mouth to stop him from shouting out - and just in time too as the front door opened.

I recognised the man before I recognised the property. He had been the one to cancel the party he'd booked for his child. He's the man who set me down this dark path of discovery. After all, had it not been for him I might still be none the wiser about the children rotting in various dumpsters. Mind you, I think there's a part of me which would have preferred not to know.

I watched, with my heart in the back of my throat, as the man looked from side to side - clearly looking for who dared pressed his doorbell in the middle of the night. Earlier he looked as though he were just arrogant but now he looked as though he were seriously angry, a face on him which suggested you'd be unwise to mess with him. He stepped back into his house and quietly closed the door so as not to wake the rest of the household (had they been fortunate enough to sleep through the initial door ringing).

"What the hell are you doing?" I hissed.

"What do you think? He's in there laughing at you and you're doing nothing about it."

"He's in there laughing at me? He's in there trying to get some fucking sleep before he has to - no doubt - get up for work in the morning!"

I climbed from the bush and started to walk back towards the van.

"What are you even doing here anyway?" he called after me.

"What do you think? You think I was going to let you out by yourself after knowing what you get up to? You're even more screwed in the head than I first believed - and, trust me, that is saying something."

I reached the van and pulled on the door handle only to find it was locked.

"Give me the keys," I told him.

"You want people laughing at you? You want people walking all over you? If you walk away now it will never stop. They'll continue treating you like the pathetic piece of shit that you are," he hissed.

"I said - give me the fucking keys."

"No. I'm not done here."

He started back towards the house. I didn't have a choice but to follow.

"What are you doing? You're messing with my life!"

He stopped a minute. "Have you ever stopped to consider you're messing with my life? You're the one who likes to dress like a fucking retard. You see me wanting to wear this shit when I leave the house? I don't fucking think so. You're making the pair of us a laughing stock and I'm not having it anymore. You understand me?" I didn't answer him. I didn't know what to say. Who could really tell who was right and who was wrong?

In my mind, I was right but in his own mind - even though it was clearly fucked - he believed he was right. He headed towards the house again.

"Just wait a minute," I begged him but he didn't listen; he just kept walking back towards the house. I physically stopped him just before he stepped onto the drive. "So what - you're going to do what here, exactly?"

"Actions speak louder than words. You're here...Come and watch."

"You know you can't get away with it forever, right? Whatever you're doing and however you go about doing it - you won't get away with it forever. They'll catch up with you."

He laughed, "With me?"

"Yes."

"I don't fucking think so," he snarled, "they'll catch up with you. You're a bad, bad man." He started to laugh and - only then - did I realise he was dressed up to look exactly like me. "I keep telling you - I'm the normal one. You're the sick one. You need help but don't you worry...When they catch up with you - and they will - I'll be there for you."

He shrugged me off and started up the drive towards the house.

I called out after him, "Please don't do this."

"I'm not. You are."

8.

I could but only watch in horror as he kicked the front door down. Two heavy kicks and it broke, allowing him the entry he desired. I looked around to see if anyone had heard the commotion. From the quick glance, it didn't look as though they had. Lights in properties nearby remained off and there was no one on the street out for a late night walk. I hurried in after him, calling out for him.

"Don't do this!" I screamed.

He didn't listen to me as he stormed through the house, charging up the stairs to the second level. I followed close by, always close by, and tried in vain to stop him but I knew now that there was no stopping him - not in this mood. I'd never seen him like this before and it was fair to say it scared the hell out of me.

"What are you doing in here?"

The father was standing by a bedroom door. I could hear his partner screaming from within the room. His earlier angry look had all but vanished from his face, replaced by a look of nervousness no doubt caused by the stranger stomping down his landing towards him.

"Call the police!" he called out to whoever was in the bedroom.

A boy - young - was screaming from another doorway across the other side of the landing. I felt sorry for him. No child should have to see this. This is the kind of thing which stays with you for life.

"Let's just go! They're calling the police!" I screamed out to him, one last-ditch attempt to stop him from doing whatever it was he planned to do. One last-ditch attempt and then I'll leave him to his own devices and get myself out of here.

"Shut the fuck up!" he screamed back to me as he swung his heavy right fist towards the father. The punch connected with a ferocity I'd never seen before, one which knocked the man down to his backside. Another punch was thrown before he started stamping his foot on the man's face. The woman in the bedroom continued to scream, frozen to the spot with fear. On the plus side, she wasn't making any emergency phone calls but I couldn't say the same for the neighbours. Within the blink of an eye, the flurry of kicks and punches were being aimed at the woman - knocking her off the bed and onto the floor in the process. Again, it didn't take long until her screams and cries fell silent leaving only the sound of the sobbing boy on the landing.

I looked to both the man and the woman - the boy's parents, their faces covered in blood and barely recognisable as human. Meanwhile, he was turning his attention to the boy.

"You know what they say about children?" he asked the petrified boy.

The boy shook his head as tears flowed freely down his face.

"Please don't do this. Come on. Let's just go before anyone phones the police. Come on..."

"If you want to go, fuck off!" he hissed. There was so much venom in his voice. I knew he wasn't going anywhere - not without doing what he came to do, whatever that was.

I looked at the boy, "I'm sorry." I couldn't be a part of this and left the two of them. Whatever he wanted to do, I couldn't stop him. I couldn't stand in his way. There was no point putting myself through it too.

II

"I think we're alone now," I spat at the boy - this fucking child who'd sooner have Iron Man at his party over a clown. In truth, I didn't give a good fuck what he had at his party. I was just using it as an excuse to hurt him. Usually I'd had to find vulnerable children to take, those who were lost or - in the case of the child at the park - abandoned as part of a 'harsh lesson' to them when they're misbehaving. Picking this kid though, this little cunt-fuck, it just made the whole process so much easier. Took out a lot of wasted time hunting around for someone suitable. "I asked you a question," I said.

"Please don't hurt me."

"I asked you a question. Allow me to repeat it. Do you know what they say about children?"

He shook his head. It was hard to know whether this was the truth or whether he was too scared to answer me. I thought 'children should be seen and not heard' was a popular saying? I could be wrong though so I won't hold it against him. Not that it makes a difference either way.

"They say children should be seen and not heard. I disagree with that. Don't think it is right. You want to know what I think the saying should be?" I asked him.

He stood there and didn't say anything. He just kept weeping like the annoying little shit that he is. He shrugged.

"I think children should not be heard. That part of the saying I agree with...But you know what else?"

"No," he whimpered.

Whiney, little, irritating shit.

"I think children should not be seen either. And you know what..."

"What?"

"You're never going to be seen again."

I dashed forward and grabbed him. He screamed a final, short scream.

III

Not for the first time I found myself pacing the lounge wearing nothing but my boxer shorts. Pretty sure - at this rate - I was going to wear a hole in my carpet. I felt sick. What he did to their faces. There was no remorse there. There was no control. He was like an animal. A rabid animal. I have to turn him in or else there'll be no stopping him. Besides, even if I don't turn him in, they'll come for him. They'll come and they'll arrest him. And me. If I don't turn him in, they'll think I am a part of what he does. I can see it now. They'll think I am just as responsible. And who could blame them? If I am innocent of it all, why would I sit back and just watch? I wouldn't. No one would.

"The washing machine would have finished by now," he said. His voice made me jump. I'd been so lost in my own thoughts I didn't realise he was there watching me. "I only put it on for a quick wash."

"What do you want? A medal?"

"I was hoping you could hang it up for us?"

"Yeah, okay."

"Really?"

"Sure - put your feet up...Tell you what - I'll get you a pedicure whilst you're at it. Maybe a nice neck massage? You've had a busy night, after all, and must be tired."

"Sarcasm doesn't suit you."

"Murdering people doesn't suit me."

"Yet you seem to have mastered it."

"I haven't killed anyone. It's all you."

"No. It's you. You're the clown. I'm the serious one. You're the one stalking the streets, you're the one snatching unhappy children. It's all you. To be fair, I hardly get out these days. Not since you keep continuing to hide me."

"Why are you doing this?"

"Which bit? Washing your outfit? Killing people?"

"Why are you trying to ruin my life?"

"You're trying to ruin mine. You're denying who I am. You're denying who you are. You need professional help, my friend."

"You're ruining my life!" I screamed back at him.

"Really? You seem to be the one who does whatever he wants. I'm just the passenger. So I get to go out and play from time to time - it's not nearly as much as I'd like to."

"Last night - all that screaming..."

"Yes - there was a fair amount..."

"Someone would have seen you."

"No, someone would have seen you. They'd have seen a clown running from the house. They'd have seen a clown backing the clown van up to the house and they'd have seen a clown running back into the house before coming back out, loading the clown van up and jumping into the front seat and speeding off...They'll have seen you."

"So you're trying to frame me?"

"You're not too bright, are you? You go down and I go down. I'm trying to survive. I'm making it so you can't go out dressed as a fucking clown anymore. The day job - it's over. Now we can go out as we're supposed to be seen. Maybe a nice suit...Maybe jeans and tee shirt. I don't know. Anything but a fucking clown outfit. Oh, and for the record if you choose to start wearing a dress to avoid me...We're having words, you understand me?" He continued, "I'm sick of you trying to hide me all of the time. Like you're better than me? Seriously? I'm the alpha here. You're the one who tags along like a pathetic, friendless little cunt."

"I won't let you get away with this," I warned him.

"You can't stop me, just as I can't stop you. All I can do is make it harder for you to be who you want to be. The fact you enjoy dressing up – well, that just makes my job that much easier, you know?"

"You're a piece of shit."

"Which technically means you're a piece of shit."

All this time hiding him under the heavy make-up of a clown, I had forgotten what he was really like. I'd forgotten the monster waiting beneath the face paint. Would people really believe I was the one responsible for his crimes?

"Your little hobby - have you been doing that just to stop me from hiding you?"

"Dear God, man, no. I've been doing that because I enjoy it. As I keep telling you, it's a great pastime. I've only just thought - these past few occasions - to use your outfit to shift the blame to you instead of me...You know - on the off-chance I do make a mistake. Like last night. I won't lie. That was sloppy."

"You're unbelievable."

"Thank you. I'll take that as a compliment."

I didn't know what to say to him. He was off the hinge. Completely mad. And now he was pulling me into his games but using my guise to his advantage and my disadvantage. Once again, I felt a sickness brewing within me. All this time I thought I was in control. Now I doubt I was ever in the driving seat. Was I always his passenger?

"Come on - stop sulking," he said. "I've got you a present. Something to say no hard feelings."

"What are you talking about?"

"Come with me. You'll like this."

The sickness brewing within me bubbled away furiously. I followed him from the living room, into the hallway and towards the kitchen. The house was silent apart from the sound of my heartbeat pumping away furiously. We stopped in the kitchen.

"Down there," he said.

The cellar door was wide open. I didn't want to go down there. I didn't want to see what he had supposedly done for me. Not after seeing what he'd previously done down there - something I wished I could forget but knew I couldn't.

"What have you done?"

He laughed. "Come on now," he said, "I think you already know what's down there, don't you?"

He wouldn't have. Would he? I tentatively walked towards the door. I cranked my head to one side in an effort to hear any kind of movement down there. Nothing. Silence, other than the sound of my own breathing.

"Come on," he said, "trust me." He gave me a nudge towards the door and suddenly stopped me, "Wait a minute...Might want to pop some clothes on. Probably best not to go down there dressed in just your boxers. First impressions and all that..."

It was then I knew for definite that we weren't alone in the house. Someone else was down there and it didn't take a genius to know who. I hurried through the downstairs of the house, to the stairs, and up to my bedroom where I quickly threw on some jeans and a tee shirt. I returned to the kitchen nervously.

"Are you ready for this?" he asked me as I stopped by the cellar door.

"No."

"Come on, you have to admit, it's all pretty exciting."

I walked through the open door and stepped down onto the first step.

"Hello?" I called out. No one answered. I flicked the basement light on and walked down the flight of rickety stairs. At the bottom, my eyes were instantly drawn to the bed in the corner of the room. More particularly - the boy lying on it. He was stripped to his underwear with a dirty gag around his mouth. Set up just in front of him was a blank canvas on one of the easels. The boy looked petrified. I ran back up the stairs and out of the room - back into the kitchen.

"What's wrong? You don't like your present?" he asked me.

"What the fuck is wrong with you? Take him back."

"No can do. Doesn't come with a receipt. No returns permitted."

"You have to let him go. If you don't, I will…"

"Not your smartest move. You let him go, he goes to the police and we both get arrested."

"I'll tell them you took him."

"And he'll tell them he saw a clown kill his mummy and daddy. All very heartbreaking…"

"We can't keep him here; we need to get rid of him."

"And that's what you're going to do. That's why I brought him back to you."

He wanted me to kill him. That much was obvious. I don't know why though. I don't know what he was trying to prove. What? Maybe that we were one and the same? We're not. I'm not a killer. I won't kill a person - let alone a child.

"Get him out of here!" I snapped at him.

He laughed, "I'm going to leave the two of you alone for a while, okay? Give you time to come to terms with the situation."

"What? Don't you fucking leave us…Hello?"

Silence.

I called out again, "Hello?"

He was gone.

I turned back to the cellar. The thought of the boy down there. What must have been going through his head? What must he have been thinking? Not just because he was down there; snatched from his home…But what he saw in his house before he was taken. He saw his mum and dad murdered before his very eyes. Is there any come back from that for him - even if I can get him out of the house?

Slowly, nervously, I made my way back to the cellar's stairs.

IV

I hesitated at the foot of the stairs. The little boy was looking at me, his eyes wide with fear - not that I expecting anything different. I smiled at him but remembered how I looked in the mirror's reflection when I was testing my grin and quickly changed my expression to a more neutral look.

"Hi," I said coyly. He didn't reply. I'm not sure whether that was because he was scared or whether it was because of the gag. I walked over to him and he flinched. "It's okay," I reassured him, "I'm not going to hurt you." Slowly, I reached down to him and removed his gag. He didn't say anything but he seemed grateful; it was in his eyes. "Is that better?" I asked him. He nodded.

"Is the clown here?" he asked.

"No. Why?"

"I don't like him," the boy said. His voice was shaking. "He scares me."

Of course the clown get-up scared him. Under the circumstances they met each other, it would have scared anyone. I felt bad for him but I also felt disappointment at his misguided fear. It wasn't the clown he should be scared of. The clown is the entertainer. The clown is the fun one.

"He's not here," I reassured him again.

"Can I go home?" he asked.

I didn't know what to say. I wanted the boy to be able to go home. Of course I did. But I knew he couldn't. For one, his parents were dead, and for another, he'd tell the police of us, and our home. I knew there was no chance of his safe return.

"Please?" he continued.

"I'll be right back." I turned away from him and hurried from the cellar, back up to the kitchen. I slammed the door shut behind me. Out of sight, out of mind.

"I wouldn't get too friendly with him," he was back, speaking in my ear. "It will only make it harder when you kill him," he continued.

"Please. I can't do it. I can't. I'm not like you…"

"…You are. You just don't know it yet."

"No. I'm not like you. I can't do it."

"Well you're going to have to."

"I can't. I won't."

"You will."

"Please. I need you to do it."

He shrugged, "I'm not going to do it for you."

"I can't do it!" I yelled.

"Then you'd better find out what he likes to eat for dinner because you've got yourself another mouth to feed." He laughed, "Good luck with that."

9.

I was hiding in my bedroom, the broken furniture still lying around from where he'd thrown it last night. I was trying to pretend none of it had happened - last night, what he did whilst wearing my outfit and the boy. I was trying and failing. Hard really - even with the door shut and him in the cellar - I could still hear him crying for his parents. I wonder if he realises they're dead? He must. He must know there is nowhere for him to go. Even if I didn't care about the police taking me - taking us - and I did let him go... Where would he run to? His life is over in more ways than one.

"You going to hide up here all day?"

"I can't just kill someone. I'm not like you."

"You like this boy?"

"I don't know him."

"Then what's the problem?"

"Just because I don't know him, it doesn't mean I want to kill him. He's a person. A human."

"He's human? Of course he is. So you're aware that - in time - he's going to die anyway. What's the problem with bringing that time forward a little?" he sneered.

"It's not my place to do so."

"Listen to him," he said. He paused long enough for me to hear the young boy crying. "He's upset. He's in pain - mentally and physically...You kill him - you're just putting him out of his misery. Keeping him alive, you're just prolonging the inevitable." He stopped talking. All I could hear was the boy's wailing. It dawned on me - what he said about a child crying - that it was annoying. Perhaps children should be seen and not heard after all. The constant screams were driving me mad. "If anything," he said, "keeping him down there, as you are, is actually crueller than killing him."

Was it crueller? Was I just delaying the inevitable? Would it be nicer just to go down there and put him out of his misery? I hated him for making me doubt my own beliefs. I hated him more than words could describe.

"Would you rather I did it?" he said finally.

"Yes."

"Well - okay. I'll do it for you."

"Thank you." It was strange to say that I felt relief for his offer yet that was exactly the feeling I had. Relief. Relief that I didn't have to kill the boy and relief that - soon - the boy would be with his mother and father, hopefully in a better place.

II

I walked over to the cupboard and pulled out one of the clown outfits hanging there. This one was red with big yellow buttons and a large white frilly collar. How the fuck he spent so much time in these things is beyond me! How did he not feel like a fucking retard?

"What are you doing?" he asked me. Jesus! Even knowing I'm the one who is going to go down and kill the boy for him, he is still talking to me in that irritating, snivelling tone of voice. I wish I could beat it out of him. Man up, for fuck's sake, you pussy.

"What do you think I'm doing? I'm getting myself dressed to go and do your dirty work."

"My dirty work? This is all down to you. If it weren't for you, he wouldn't even be here. If it weren't for you, his parents would..."

"Shut the fuck up. You're like a broken record. Take some fucking responsibility in your life once in a while." I stepped into the clown suit and zipped myself in. There. I look like a fucking dick.

"Why the outfit?"

"You'd rather I go down and kill him without it? It's no skin off my nose. I'm wearing this for you. You think I want to be wearing it? Because I don't."

"You're wearing it for me?"

"This look is tainted - the whole clown outfit...After what happened last night. You know it is. You think you'll ever be able to dress in it again? You know - without thinking of what happened? Because I don't think you will. This way, the killings are confined to the clown outfit as far as you're concerned and the look you have when you're not dressed like a pillock...Well...That's the good look, the safe look - the look where you haven't actually witnessed anyone die. You see what I mean?" He looked confused - as though he didn't understand how the 'normal' look (without all of the make-up) was suddenly the look which felt safe, and the one he'd hidden behind for all these years was the one he associated with murder and mayhem. I smiled. He'll never be able to put this suit on again. He'll never be able to hide me again. I have stolen his identity. I looked to the floor where I'd thrown the make-up table. Various make-up products and face paints were scattered around next to it. I walked over to them and picked it up. "You going to at least help me put this shit on so it looks the part?"

III

We were standing in the upstairs bathroom, looking into the dirty mirror (part of the medicine cabinet hanging on the wall). I was applying the white face paint with one of the sponges he'd picked up for me. I was on auto-pilot, not really listening to what he was saying, a feeling of sadness that the outfit I had been hiding behind had forever been marred with what he'd done last night in his fit of rage or revenge, whatever the hell it was that drove him to do that.

"When you were a kid - did you ever have the tendency to wear make-up? I only ask because you're pretty good at putting it on."

When I was a 'kid' as he put it, I was living in relative peace. He hadn't been a part of my life. Not when I was young. He only came to live with me when I hit my teens. He was relatively quiet to start off with. The occasional whisper in my ear after my pa had visited me in one of his many drunken (horny) states.

"You going to let him get away with that?" he'd ask me as I wept into my pillow, a trickle of father's so-called love running down between my legs. "I wouldn't. I'd fucking kill him. We can - if you want. We can do it together. I'll take your hand, I'll show you how."

He only got louder when I ignored him. His hatred towards my dad turned to hatred towards me;,especially when I cried. He'd call me pathetic and worthless. He'd say I deserved everything I got. I tried to block him from my mind. I tried to make sure I didn't hear any of his words but they only got louder. By the time I was in my late teens he was practically impossible to ignore - and soon it wasn't just me that he was talking to.

"You fucking touch him again and I'll kill you," I heard him say to Dad once. Dad responded by hitting him. I screamed for Dad to stop but he carried on until his hands were too sore. Soon after, I moved out of the house I shared with Dad. I never spoke to him again. Soon after, he was dead - beaten in the back alley of a pub with no witnesses. I wasn't alone. He went with me. At first I was glad for the company. He kept telling me that everything was going to be okay if I stuck with him. He said he'd look after the pair of us but he was always quick to temper.

I stopped applying the make-up and stared into the mirror. He stared back.

"What?"

"Did you kill him?"

"Who?"

"Did you kill Dad?"

He smiled at me. That was his answer. Words weren't needed.

"Did he suffer?"

He gave me a wink, "It was about as uncomfortable as things were made for you when you were growing up."

"What happened?"

"I hit him with a brick." He said it so matter-of-fact that it made me nervous. There was no emotion there. No empathy, no guilt, nothing. Which is exactly what I felt too. He smiled at me. "He begged for his life as he lay there on the floor, shell-shocked. He stopped begging by the fourth hit."

I realised then - when he was talking to me - that it wasn't him who was smiling at me but, for the first time ever, I was smiling at him.

"Thank you," I said. I went back to applying the various face paints. He didn't say anything. I think the both of us were shocked at my gratitude. I know I was, but to know he did that for me - killed my dad, the man who made me suffer as I grew up behind locked doors...Maybe he had my back after all?

"I'm going to cut him," he said after a few more minutes of blissful peace.

"What? Who?"

"The boy downstairs. That's how I'm going to do it."

I swallowed hard. I wasn't sure whether I wanted to hear the details. I wasn't going to go in the room with him; I was going to leave him to it.

"I want to know how long it will take for someone to bleed out from their asshole."

"What?"

"That's where I'm putting the blade. Never done it before but always been curious about it."

"You can't. That's cruel."

"You think I'm nice to the people I've had down there?"

"Can't you make it quick for him?" I begged.

"For all we know, it might be quick."

"I meant - suffocate him or something? Something, I don't know, a little more humane?"

He smiled at me and leaned in close to the mirror until we were practically touching, "You're welcome to do it yourself?"

Any thanks I felt towards him - for what he did to my father - soon disappeared. I was backed into a corner. I didn't have a choice but to do it myself. Not if I wanted the boy to die without unnecessarily suffering.

"I'll do it," I sighed.

"Attaboy!"

IV

I was standing in the kitchen staring ahead at the cellar door. The wig was in place, the outfit was on and I knew what had to be done, yet I wasn't thinking about it. My mind was on how we had got to this stage. Everything had happened so fast. I was a children's entertainer. I was doing okay with my job. I enjoyed it. No, I loved it. And now - I'm an accomplice to murders (God knows how many exactly), and I feel as though my personality has been pulled in the direction of his own. A darker and more uncomfortable path - one I wish I could turn away from but...Like I said, I don't know how I have ended up here.

"You're going to make it harder for yourself," he said to me. His voice wasn't snappy. If anything, he sounded as though he were trying to be genuinely helpful. Was he? Or was this another trick? Had he even been tricking me? Had he been pulling me in this direction or was I heading there anyway? "The longer you wait," he continued, "the harder it will be to follow through with."

"I'm not sure I can do this," I told him. "I need to think about it."

"Making it harder. Not just for you. For him too."

"I..."

"You just need to get down there and do it. Trust me."

I reached out for the handle and stopped myself from grabbing it. I pulled my hand away.

"Five minutes and it will all be over," he pushed.

"I don't want you to come down there with me," I said. "I need to do this by myself." By going down alone, it still left me the possibility to leave without hurting the boy. At least, not hurting him anymore than I'd already done so. Why am I blaming myself? It wasn't me. It was him. Just because he was dressed like me. Wait...That's it... I'll explain to the boy what happened and then...I can let him go and if he does go to the police (and I'm sure he will), he'll explain I'm the innocent one.

"I'll give you your time," he said.

"Thank you." Another 'thanks'? It was beginning to become a habit.

"Any ideas how you're going to do it?" he asked.

I shook my head. He had spoken of cutting him but I knew I wouldn't be able to do that. I didn't have it in me to push a knife through someone's skin, hard enough to penetrate organs. The mere thought of doing so repulsed me.

"I'll think of something," I said.

I waited by the stairs as he made himself scarce. When I was sure he'd gone, I stepped onto the first step and slowly made my way down. The kid screamed when he saw me; I'd made it halfway down the stairs before he did so. I continued down the stairs until I was on the same level with him. I turned to him and put my hands up to show I wasn't carrying anything, "It's okay," I told him. "I don't want to hurt you." The boy burst into tears. I slowly walked over to where he was lay. He fidgeted on the mattress, straining to get away from me. "Please don't," I asked him. I was trying to keep my voice quiet, calm - soothing almost - but I don't think the tone mattered. I don't think he heard the tone. Looking at his panicked expression, I'm not sure if he is hearing the words either. "I don't want to hurt you," I told him. "I won't hurt you. I just want to talk to you."

To try and relax him a little, I stepped a little further back from him. Maybe my proximity was causing him more distress. I noticed some of the paintings would have been visible from where he was lying on the bed. No wonder he was so upset; they probably scared the hell out of him. I turned them around so he couldn't see them anymore.

"They're not mine," I told him as I turned the last of the paintings around. "They're his."

There was a chair standing in the corner of the room. I walked over to it and perched myself on it. The pair of us fell into an uncomfortable silence, neither of us knowing what to say for the best. For a brief moment I contemplated putting on a show for him. Not sure what exactly. According to his dad, he didn't want a clown at his party. He wanted Iron Man. Did that mean he hated clowns and what we do? Or was it more to do with just preferring Iron Man? Maybe he loves clowns? Yes. He loves them but opted for Iron Man because he thought his friends would prefer that. An unselfish act on his part. He doesn't deserve to die. I ran through the performance possibilities in my head wondering what he'd prefer: a balloon animal or a card trick? Maybe a few jokes? Jesus. I don't know. I don't know anything about this kid. Other than the fact he saw his mum and dad stamped to death.

I broke the silence and cut straight to the chase, "Do you recognise me?" I asked.

He nodded.

"That's good." He realised I was the man who'd previously spoken to him down here, before going away and putting this costume on. That might mean he realises it wasn't me standing in his house. It wasn't me and - more importantly - that it was him pretending to be me.

"You were in my house."

My heart sank.

"You hurt my mum and dad," he started to cry again.

"No - you see - that's what I wanted to talk to you about. It wasn't me. It was him. He was dressed as me."

"No, it was you."

"It wasn't. I promise. I wouldn't want to hurt you. I wouldn't want to hurt anyone."

"You hurt my mum and dad," he said again, tears streaming down his face.

"No. You're not listening. It was him. He dressed up like me so I would get the blame for it but - and I promise - it wasn't me at all. It wasn't. I'm not like that. I'm on your side..."

"What the hell are you doing?" a harsh voice cut in making me jump.

"I told you not to come down here," I hissed.

"I asked you a question. What the fuck do you think you're doing? What are you saying?"

"Nothing. I wasn't saying anything."

The boy looked both confused and scared. I tried to give him a look - a quick glance to let him know I'm here and I'm on his side - just as I had promised to him only seconds earlier.

"Why are you trying to make fucking friends with the little cunt? You're down here to kill him. Why the fuck are you making things complicated for yourself? No. Not just yourself...Complicated for both of us. What? You a selfish cunt, is that it?"

"You're being over the top. You've got the wrong end of the stick..."

"Have I fuck. I was here, listening. I heard it all. You're trying to tell him you're the innocent one..."

"No. I wasn't saying..."

"Don't you fucking lie to me."

"I'm not!"

"Please stop it!" the boy cried out as he pulled against his restraints.

"I swear to God I'm not!" I said, ignoring the boy.

"Then prove it! Finish him!"

There was no way the boy was getting out of there alive. I should have just stormed over to him and done what was required but I couldn't move. My feet were rooted to the spot. I couldn't help but think of the boy as a life. It wasn't mine to take, no matter what it meant if he got away. So what if I go to prison? Perhaps I deserve it? I should have just turned the pair of us in as soon as I realised what he was doing in his own time. Jesus - how could I have been so blind to it? All this time, right under my own nose - a fucking murderer!

"You're fucking weak! You're a disgrace. A fucking coward!" he screamed at me, a rage in his voice I'd not heard before. I could only watch as he stormed towards the boy. "If you want a job done..."

V

"...Do it yourself!" I yelled. The child screamed as I approached him. Quite right too; I'm not a pussy like that prick. I pulled the pillow out from under his head and promptly muffled his scream by placing it over his squirming face.

"Get off him!"

"Why? Are you going to finish this fucking thing?"

"Just get off him."

I tried to pull him away but he shook me off.

"I will kill you!" he hissed. "As soon as I'm done with him, I will fucking kill you if you touch me again. Do you understand me?"

VI

The boy's limbs were flailing around underneath his weight. I could only watch in horror as I became witness to another death. I started to gag. Soon, the boy's limbs went limp and yet he still didn't climb off from him. He waited there, on top of him, with the pillow over the boy's face as though making sure he was definitely gone.

"Get off him," I begged.

"Fine."

He got off the boy and dropped the pillow to the floor. I saw the boy's face - pale with lifeless eyes - and couldn't hold in the sick anymore. I ran to the corner of the room and threw up on the floor.

"I know I keep saying it but - really - you are a fucking joke. An absolute joke."

I started to weep; not because of what he was saying, but because there - in the corner of the room - was another dead boy.

"Get the fuck out of my sight whilst I finish up down here!"

I didn't need him to ask me twice and promptly left.

10

I kicked the clown outfit off and threw it towards the washing machine where the other one was already soaking, post-service. With the outfit off, I leaned into the sink and threw up again. I'm glad he was preoccupied so he didn't witness that. He already thought badly of me. Badly? That was a joke. The way he was talking to me, I thought he was going to kill me as soon as the boy was disposed of. I'm still worried he may try.

I ran the tap water into the sink to wash the vomit down the plughole; whilst doing so, I looked towards the cellar. I'm not sure how to fix this. I'm not sure how to make all of this go away. All I know is that he's tainted my way of living beyond repair. I feel as though he has destroyed me. Another bubble from my stomach. Hold it in. Hold it in. Don't be a pussy. Am I being sick because of what I've witnessed these past few days or because of stress - worry about what he's going to say (or do) to me? He might not be able to kill me but he has already proven he can make things awkward for me. And what if he does figure out a way to kill me? Would he? I know - if I could - I'd end his life.

"I think we need to talk!"

His voice made me jump. I caught sight of him in the kitchen window's reflection, a look of pure hatred in his eyes. Wait. No. Is that hatred? It's not. It's not the same look I've seen on him before. It's something else. What is that? That's it. I know it. Disappointment. My dad used to look at me like that on nights I failed to please him.

"I thought we had reached an understanding?"

It didn't matter if his tone did match his expression (definitely disappointment), I still found myself feeling nervous of him. For the first time ever, I realised I was actually scared of him. You can't blame me; I had witnessed him murder people and I know there are more that he has killed.

"What? You not talking to me now? The silent treatment?" he pressed me further.

"I can't understand you."

"You can't understand me? Why ever not? I'm probably the easiest person to understand..."

"No. I can't understand how you can kill people."

"It's easy. Think about it."

"I have thought about it. Ever since you showed me that bag...I can't get my head around it. I can't. It's not the right thing to do."

"Says who?"

"Society."

"What if society is wrong and I am right? Have you ever thought of that?" He took a breath, "I want to show you something."

"I don't want to see it." I had seen enough of what he wanted to show me. Whatever it was he had for me to see this time, I didn't want to know.

"It's not really an option," he whispered.

Before I could answer, he dragged me back down to the cellar. I fought with him as he pulled me towards the bed where the small boy still lay. When we were close enough, he forced me to look upon it. The poor boy staring dead ahead - was he looking at me?

"Please let me go," I begged him. I didn't want to be seeing this. I wanted nothing to do with it. He knew this, so why was he forcing me to see it? He knows I'm not the same as him. I don't have it in me.

"Look at him," he whispered in my ear. He no longer sounded as though he was disappointed, nor angry. He sounded very 'matter-of-fact'. "You remember how much pain he was in?" he asked. "You remember how upset he was?"

"Of course I do," I said.

"Do you remember the pain in his eyes?"

"Yes."

"How much pain was there?" he asked.

"A lot."

"A lot. Yes. Now look."

Again, he forced me to look the boy in his eyes.

"What do you see now?" he continued.

I tried to relax a little. I realised I wasn't going to get away with not looking. I had to go along with whatever it was he was trying to show me. Besides, the sooner I went along with it, the sooner he might let me go about my own business (which was anything other than this). I looked at the boy more closely but I wasn't sure what I was supposed to be looking at.

"Do you see it?" he pushed me for an answer.

"I don't know what I'm supposed to be seeing," I said.

"In his eyes."

I shrugged, "I...don't...."

"Peace. He looks peaceful."

I looked in the boy's eyes again. There was no pain, there was no fear, there was nothing - in that respect, I guess there was peace.

"He's not crying anymore," he said. "There's no stress, there's no worry, there's nothing - just absolute peace. Now, do you remember a time when you've ever seen that much peace in someone's eyes?"

I shook my head, "No."

"That's right. No." He continued, "It's nice, isn't it?"

I wondered whether he believed any of what he was actually saying or whether it was just for my benefit. He walked over to one of the easels and slid a blank canvas onto it. Once in place, he reached for a small paint brush from a pot of various painting implements. I watched in silence as he started to outline what looked to be the boy.

"Don't you wish you could feel peace like this?" he asked, with a nod of his head towards the boy.

"Yes."

"Yes. Do you think any of us will ever feel peace like that?"

I shook my head.

"I can't hear you."

"No."

"No," he agreed. "You see those pictures over in the corner of the room as souvenirs from lives I have taken, but I see it differently. I see it as children I have given peace to."

I didn't say anything as he continued to paint the dead child. I just stood with him, in silence, as I contemplated what he had said, wondering whether he believed it or whether he was simply trying to turn me into his way of thinking - and the 'peace' theory just so happened to work in his favour.

He stopped painting, "Sorry - did you want to give this a go?" he asked. "It's very therapeutic."

"No. No, thank you."

"Suit yourself," he said as he resumed what he was doing.

I looked at the painting. At first, I thought he was going to draw everything in front of us but - with each little stroke of the brush - it was becoming apparent that this particular picture was going to be of the young boy's eyes only.

II

The same thought kept racing through my mind as I sat in the living room, leaving him to whatever else he wanted to do; he is killing people because he believes he is giving them the peace they deserve, the peace they long for. I knew it was still wrong, regardless of how you dressed it up but - when you looked at it like that - it wasn't as bad as I first believed it to be. I mean, he isn't necessarily a cold-hearted murderer. He is a man on a mission of mercy. I wonder, would the police go easy on him if they knew the truth? What if I phoned them up and told them? Would they go easy on both of us? I looked across to the telephone which sat on a small coffee table next to the sofa. Whilst he's busy, I should phone them. It's the right thing to do. Surely he'll see that when they come for him? Wait a minute, no. They won't see it like that. They can't. The boy is at peace now but they'll argue he was at peace before he was taken from his home. He was at peace before he saw his mum and dad killed. Shit. What a tangled web we weave. As my mind raced with various thoughts it stuck on one in particular, something he'd said to me when he first showed me what he had done. Something about children being bastards, or cunts. I can't remember the exact words he used. There was more. Something about children being seen and not heard...The child in the park - he said he was doing the mum a favour by getting rid of the kid. There was no mention of giving the child the peace he yearned for. Everything he'd said to me, in the cellar, was just bullshit and - again - I'd been suckered in by it. Fuck.

I reached my hand out but went past the phone. I grabbed the controller instead. Thoughts of the child in the park - I'd been so busy with what happened last night...Had they found the boy yet? Did they have any leads on what happened?

I flicked the television on via the controller and started hopping through the channels. So many channels. I'm sure the last time I paid any attention to the TV there were only four. When did there become so many? And, more to the point, why can't I find what I'm looking for on any of them? Chat show, chat show, chat show (how many chat shows?), soap, some shitty made-for-television film with piss poor acting and a distinct lack of any serious direction…No news.

The clock on the front of my DVD player showed it to be coming up to midday. There must be something coming on the channels soon. I'll just sit and wait. Ignoring the child in the park for a moment, I need to know if the bodies from last night have been discovered and, more to the point, whether there were any witnesses or not.

"Regardless," his voice made me jump again. I wished he would stop jumping out on me. "You might want to hide the van, just to be safe…" A feeling of panic rushed through me. I hadn't given much thought to the van. It was hardly the most inconspicuous vehicle out there. It wouldn't have been hard for someone to spot it at the crime scene. Either crime scene.

"You realise they probably already know about us?" I said. My voice was quiet. Downbeat. "Someone would have seen the van. It'll only be a matter of time before the police come knocking on the door, asking all sorts of questions."

"Then you'd better think of an alibi," he said, "but if I were you, I wouldn't say you were with me."

"What if they come here with search warrants?" I asked as I started to panic. Before the investigation for what happened last night was possibly even open, my brain was telling me it was already over for us. If they came here, with papers, they'd find the cellar (no hiding it) and they'd find not only the boy's body but also the paintings of the other children. Even if I told them they weren't real - just the product of a diseased mind - I doubt they'd believe me.

"You think I haven't already thought about that?" he asked. "Do you take me for an amateur?"

"Look, I'm sorry, but all of this is kind of new to me."

"Go back down to the cellar."

"I don't want to. I've seen the fucking cellar," I snapped at him. Snapping was a mistake. It served no other purpose than to anger him and he barked - once again - for me to go down to the cellar before dragging me down there against my own will.

I couldn't believe what I saw when we made it to the bottom of the stairs. The room was a mess, yes, but…There were no signs of anything untoward happening down here. The bed was leaning on its side against the far wall as though it had been abandoned by previous owners of the home - certainly easier than disposing of it themselves and certainly nothing to raise any suspicions. The cellar was clearly a dumping ground for junk just as attics were used for similar. I continued to look around. The paintings were missing too. Where they'd previously been leaning in a neat mile, there was nothing but dust on the floor. Even the damned easels were missing. Had they ever been here? Was it all just a figment of my imagination when I'd earlier seen it down here?

"What the fuck are you talking about?" he laughed.

"Am I losing my mind?" I asked him. If I were to drive to the boy's house and knock on the door, would his mum and dad answer? The pair of them perfectly unharmed? Would the boy come to the top of the stairs to see who was calling on them? Maybe hopeful it was his one of his friends coming around to invite him out? Was everything that happened recently all in my damaged mind? I felt a piece of hope flow through me. That was, at least, until he opened his trap again.

"Look in the other corner," he laughed. He turned my head towards the darkest corner of the room. "Look at the floor."

There was a freshly dug (and re-covered) hole.

"The boy?"

"The boy."

"And the pictures?"

"Of course not. You know what the rotting flesh will do to the paint? I need them hidden, not completely ruined." He turned my head towards the wall opposite to where the bed leaned. Bricks. I looked closely in the dim light. They'd been disturbed too. Not all of them. Just enough of them. Enough of them to make a small hiding hole for, I'm guessing, the pictures.

"You've been busy," I said. I'd so wished my mind was damaged beyond all boundaries of sanity. I'd rather that, if it meant the boy and his family (and the other children) were alive. My mind is damaged beyond all repair but not in a way which allowed me any peace. They were dead and he was very much in control as to what happened between us. All these years, I thought I was in the driving seat but no, it's him. It has always been him.

"Like I said," he continued, "you need to think about what you're going to say should the police come. And, more importantly, you need to get rid of that van...I've done my bit. You do your bit. For once. Understand?"

He left me standing there in the cellar, so he could go and rest up, with so many thoughts buzzing through my head, only one really loud one though: the nagging doubt that I'll have it in me to throw anyone off the scent of what we have done here. I'm not a good liar. I always go red. I squirm. It's uncomfortable and I hate it. Even now I'm starting to feel my face burn up at the prospect of having to lie to someone, let alone someone as important as a police officer. I know I can't. I'll let us down. I'll let him down. He'll be angry with me. Again. He'll never let me live it down if I ruin things for us. He'll continue to plague me with his beliefs about what is right and what is wrong, always ignoring my own thoughts.

Something he'd said when forcing me to look the dead boy in the eyes popped into my thoughts, specifically a question he'd asked. He asked whether either of us would feel the peace the boy felt in his death. I'd said no. I didn't feel we could feel the same level of peace he felt and it tore me apart inside. The knowledge that I'll never be as happy as other people I bump into in my life. I'll never have that feeling of satisfaction they have with their lives. I tried to think what I had done to deserve such a life. Why had I deserved such misery and pain and suffering? What had I done that was so bad? Even at a young age, when I was living with Dad, I was being seemingly punished and for what? Why? I was just a normal kid trying to live my life. I didn't ask for what happened. And then he showed up in my life. I didn't ask for him to come by and I certainly didn't ask for him to get involved with Dad. He simply took it upon himself to do so and now he expected me to be grateful for it? It was unfair.

I left the cellar via the stairs and entered the kitchen. I'm never going to be happy. I know that. Why should I keep trying to live a life like this? It's not good for either of us. And now his murderous impulses are out in the open, it's clearly not good enough for other people either. I don't want to live like this. Not with him. Especially when we're taken into custody. A lifetime spent rotting in a cell with only his hostile company? No. That's not for me...

I stormed over to the kitchen worktop and pulled a knife from one of the drawers. I held it firmly in my right hand and pressed the tip of the blade against my shaking wrist. It will hurt. I know that. But it will only do so for a moment. A moment of pain for the same blissful feeling the children were rewarded with. I want that. I want what they found in their death. I want what he gave them. I pushed down a little harder. A small trickle of blood appeared where the tip of the blade had pierced my skin. It stung but not in a bad way. If anything, with all my pent-up feelings, I felt a bit of a release.

He pulled the knife away from me and threw it across the room. I watched on, helplessly, as it penetrated the cellar door and stuck in the wood.

"What the fuck are you doing?" he hissed at me.

"I thought you'd gone. I thought I was alone!"

"You're trying to kill yourself? Is that it? What - you want to fucking die?"

"I don't want to live. I want the peace."

"You're a coward."

"No I'm not."

"Yes you are. You won't face your responsibilities. You're a fucking coward. You think there is a peace to be found by taking your own life? There's not. Eternal damnation waits for those who die by their own hand."

"We're damned anyway, thanks to you."

"I won't let you kill yourself. I won't let you kill us."

"Please..."

I tried to cross the kitchen to where the knife was stuck in the door but he stopped me. For the first time ever, I realised he was actually stronger than me. It never used to be like that. We used to be equal but these last couple of days were really starting to take it out of me.

"No."

"I don't want to live like this," I begged him.

"You don't have a choice."

"I can't live like this."

"I'll make you."

"Please..." I tried again to lunge for the knife but - again - he stopped me. With the feeling of despair at how weak I felt, I wanted to scream.

"Not got much fight in you, have you? Fucking pussy."

I watched helplessly as he sauntered over to the knife and pulled it from the door. He laughed as he waved in front of my face, "Is this the knife you wanted? It's nice. I can see why you picked this one. Fucking sharp. Do some damage with this."

"Fuck you."

"Fuck me? No. Fuck you. You tried to kill us both because you're too much of a pussy to carry on? Fucking selfish, not forgetting weak and pathetic."

I tried again to take the knife from him but he kept it from my reach, even laughing at my attempts to regain control. He slammed the knife down into the worktop so that it was sticking out from the wooden top, a cheap version of the sword in the stone.

"You want to play with knives?" he hissed. "Fine - let's play with knives."

He reached down to the washing machine and yanked the door open.

"What are you doing?" I asked as he pulled the now clean, but still damp, clown outfit from within.

"We're going out."

"No. Okay. I'm sorry. You're right. I'm pathetic. I'm a pussy. Let's just stay in. We can work something out..." I begged as he started kicking his clothes off.

"Every time I've talked to you,   you've ignored me or tried to go behind me back. And to think, you believe I am the evil one. You need your head examining."

"Well you haven't exactly been upfront with me. You don't want to offer the children a peace they're missing from life - you just want them dead."

"Well...True...But - hey - it was a white lie to make you feel better about yourself. You, on the other hand, are just destructive," he sneered. He slid the cold, damp clown outfit on. "How do I look?"

"Take it off. Put your normal clothes back on. Let's go and have a conversation."

"I would but...So many people to kill. I just don't have the time."

He reached out, grabbed the knife and stormed from the kitchen. I followed, knowing I was powerless to stop him from doing whatever it was he had planned. He grabbed a pair of trainers from a cupboard under the stairs and stepped into them before grabbing the wig from the stairs - where it was always abandoned. He got to the door and reached for the handle.

"Please..." I tried one last-ditch attempt to stop him.

"Do you really want to die?" he asked. His voice seemed to have less hatred in it.

"It was a mistake. A moment of weakness."

He smiled, "You're lying. Again. You want to talk and yet you always lie. You can't help yourself."

"Fine. I want to die. I want peace. I want what the children have. You know, the ones you killed..."

"I won't be able to watch you all the time," he said.

He was right. No matter how strong he believed he was, there was no way he'd be able to watch me all the time. There'd be times where he wouldn't be with me and - as soon as that time came - I'd do what needed to be done. I would end my life and find the peace I sought.

He smiled again. I felt unnerved.

"I'm not ready to die," he said, his voice cold and low. "And so, we have a problem."

"It appears so."

"That's all I needed to know. Thank you."

He reached out for the door handle, twisted it, pulled the door open and stepped out of the house. He slammed the door shut. My mind was panicking as to what was going through his own mind. He was up to something.

11.

I opened the van's door and jumped in, throwing the knife onto the passenger seat. This fucking vehicle.

"Where are you going? What are you planning? Tell me!" he was still bleating in my ear like the little bitch that he was. I wanted to tell him to shut the fuck up but I didn't. I managed to restrain myself as I fired up the engine; another cloud of black smoke spewed from the back of the van.

I leaned across to the satnav system and starting going through the recent additions to various postcodes he has visited as part of his job. The one at the top of the list was where I'd taken the boy from. The one underneath - that boy whose father wanted to play the hero -he'll do.

"What are you fucking doing?" he screeched like a wild banshee when he saw I had selected the postcode. I ignored him as I sat back in the seat and reached for the seat belt. "Whatever you're planning...Please don't. Please. I'm begging you. Whatever you want, I'll do it."

I glared at him via the rear-view mirror, "I can't ever leave you without fearing you're going to do something stupid so, really, you haven't left me much choice."

"I won't do anything. I won't. I promise. Let's just go home."

"I don't think so."

I selected reverse gear and backed out of the driveway, onto the main road. The gearstick slipped through to first and I slammed on the accelerator, not that this van was particularly quick at pulling away but still...

"What are you going to do?"

I looked to the knife and smiled. Did he really need me to spell it out? Out of the corner of my eye I could see that he wanted to snatch the knife from the chair so I reached across and took a hold of it. I put it on my lap, just to reiterate it's my knife. Not his.

"You won't get away with it!" He sounded desperate now.

"I don't plan to."

"Then why are you doing it?"

"Because I don't want to die. I can't trust you not to do anything stupid so you've left me one option...Get all of my killing out of my system today, tonight, and then turn us in."

"They'll throw away the key..."

"That's right so I'd better really make an impact tonight," I laughed.

"But what's the point? They'll never let us out..."

"Exactly. And when I tell them of your suicidal tendencies, they'll never let you out of their sight either. You won't be able to wipe your arse without them watching, let alone kill yourself."

"You're throwing away your freedom."

"Freedom, yes. But I am saving my own life."

"This is fucking ridiculous!"

"Said the man who wanted to take his own life. Just shut the fuck up and enjoy the ride," I snapped. I leaned down to the radio and turned it up to its full volume to drown out his whining voice. He wanted to die, I wanted to live. The way I saw it, this was the only option I had: have one great day and night - a time to really build some strong memories - and then spend the rest of my time in a small cell replaying those memories whilst ignoring his pathetic bleating. It may not sound ideal but I'd sooner live a life like that than not live a life at all.

He screamed over the sound of The Animals' tune "House of the Rising Sun" blasting from the van's crackling speakers, "You won't even get to your destination! The police will see the van and they'll pull you over! You said yourself last night was sloppy!"

He was getting desperate now. Yes, there was a chance that he was right - the police could pull us over before we got to where we needed to be but I figured it was a slim chance. Certainly worth risking, considering what was bubbling away in my dark thought processes.

I turned down another road. Despite the time, traffic was relatively sparse. I was quite thankful about that. The last thing I wanted to do was find myself sitting in a jam with this whining son of a bitch.

"You're being a fucking idiot," he screamed.

I always found it funny when he swore and couldn't help but laugh. For some reason, it just didn't suit his tone of voice and, instead of sounding threatening, he sounded like he was desperately trying to be one of the cool kids. Well - whatever - as long as he is ranting and raving instead of trying to get in my way, he can do whatever the fuck he wants. I don't need to listen.

We continued to drive for about twenty minutes until I eventually pulled up outside of the house I'd been aiming for. I can't remember the name of the kid and I can't remember the name of the dad who so desperately wanted to be seen as a hero in front of his son. I had been pretty excited ever since leaving the house because of what I had planned to do but now we were sitting outside of the guy's actual house, I was fucking buzzing: a grin stretching from ear to ear, a pleasant tingling sensation rushing through my very being. I killed the engine and - in doing so - the radio. The sound of (near) silence. My ears were ringing. Not sure whether that was because of the radio's previous volume or whether he'd been constantly panicking and flapping in them.

He tried one last time, "Please, I'm begging you, don't do this."

"Hush now." I snatched the knife from my lap and kicked open the driver's door.

I hopped down and looked around. Relatively quiet. Not that I would have given a fuck if it hadn't been. I stomped my way from van to house and knocked heavily on the door. Little pig, little pig - let me in...

"I don't want to see this," he said, his voice audibly quivering.

"And yet you stay here with me."

We could hear footsteps from the other side of the door. I slid the knife into the oversized pocket of his suit. A second later and the door opened. A woman was standing there with a bemused look upon her face. What? She never seen a clown before?

"Can I help you?" she asked.

"I'm here to see the birthday boy!" I said. I tried to sound jolly but I think I came across as loud. Need to try and camp it up a bit so I can sound a little more like him, the pathetic faggot. He was trying to talk, trying to warn her, but I managed to keep him quiet with a little concentration on my part.

"Johnny?" she asked.

Johnny, that was the fucker! And his dad's name was Colin. Cunty Colin. I remember now. Not that I'd bothered to speak to either of them when we were last here. Fuck getting involved with that shit. I let him do all the talking back then.

"Oh it's you! You did his party!" she said, a look of sudden realisation on her face as though she'd solved the world's greatest mystery. I wanted to deny it - tell her it wasn't me who'd performed at the party - but I couldn't. I knew that would just cause problems by confusing her. "What can I do for you?" she asked, seemingly more at ease now.

"Is Johnny in?" I asked, trying to keep it light. "I have a present for him that I forgot to give to him at his party?"

"Really? Oh wow! He'll be so excited to see you. He was talking about you for days," she said. She stepped back a bit and opened the door wider for me. Does she really think I'm that fat? Cheeky whore. Can't say she'll live to regret that moment of rudeness. I thanked her (because I'm polite) and stepped into the house. She closed the door behind me.

"Johnny?" she called up the stairs, "You have a visitor!"

"Who is it?" came the squeaky voice of a runt.

Kids aren't just annoying because they're whiney and selfish, throwing temper tantrums when they don't get what they believe they deserve... A lot of the reasons they're generally annoying is down to their voices. Slightly higher pitched than they need to be - one octave away from being audible to nearby dogs only. They just kind of squeak at you when they speak. And some of them have the need to touch you when they're talking too, probably because they know you're not really listening. They come up to you and just tap you whilst saying what they think they need to say. You, in turn, stand there and listen to them - even if you were in the middle of a conversation with a friend or partner - because you know it's the quickest way to get them to fuck off. Oops. Footsteps at the top of the landing. Happy face on.

Johnny's face beamed when he saw me. My face beamed too, despite wanting to kick his fucking head in right there and then. Him and his rude mother. A quiet voice was yelling at me in my head to tell me to behave, ordering me to get out of the house. Not going to happen.

"Hi, kiddo!" I yelled enthusiastically.

I turned to his mother, "Colin due home?"

"He'll be home in a couple of hours," she said. She looked just as thrilled as her son. I somehow think that was more to do with his reaction at seeing me than seeing me for herself, especially going by the look on her face when she first opened the front door to me.

"That's a shame," I said, "he'll miss your death…"

"I'm sorry?" she turned to me, a sudden look of terror in her eyes. Before she could react further, or even have the time to scream, I pulled the knife from my pocket and stuck it into her throat. Her eyes bulged in both pain and fear as a smile spread across my thin lips and a scream burst from dear little Johnny. I pulled the knife from her throat to a satisfying spray of blood and an audible gargle. She dropped to her knees, clutching frantically at the wound as her son about-turned and charged back up the stairs. Silly little Johnny. The front door would have been a safer option for him: less chance of me catching him before he finds sanctuary with an alarmed neighbour.

I stepped over his mother's body as she continued to writhe around in pain. She wouldn't last much longer, going by the blood pumping from her scrawny throat. At the bottom of the stairs I shouted up to my new best friend, "Johnny! Where are you going? We have two hours of playtime before Daddy is home...Don't you want to make the most of it?" I laughed as I started my way up the stairs.

II

I was desperate to do something to help them but was powerless. What was wrong with me? Why couldn't I regain control and take charge of the situation? Why am I letting him control me like this?

"You've had some fun, I get it. You're in control..." I tried telling him. I wasn't sure whether he wasn't hearing me or whether he was ignoring me. It didn't even matter if I was shouting at him.

"Johnny!" He was walking up the stairs, calling out the boy's name in a low voice."Johhhhhhhhnny.....Johhhhhhhhhnnnnnnnnnnnnnnyyyyyyyyyyy.....Got a little pressie for ya!" He stopped at the top of the stairs and looked down the landing for any sign of movement. "Come here, Johhhhhhhhnny, time to play a little game..." I watched, desperate to reach out and stop him, as he tapped the bloodied knife on the side of his face as he weighed up his options with regards to which room to try first.

"You can't do this, please..."

"Oh, hush your mouth," he hissed at me, the first time he has responded to me in what seems to be an age. I seized the opportunity to keep him talking - maybe long enough for help to come (Colin returning home, perhaps?) – just to keep the boy alive.

"We have to go home. Let's go home and talk things through. I promise - I won't try and kill myself again. I'll do whatever you want. I'll even let you keep control, at all times. I won't interfere. Please. I promise. You have to believe me. Just let the boy live.

There was a mirror hanging from the longest wall of the landing. He looked into it - at my reflection - and slowly raised his finger to his lips.

"Ssh!"

III

I turned my attention back to where little Johnny could possibly be hiding. No way out from up here - at least not without jumping from the window or running back down the stairs and I can't see him doing either.

What I like about little children is that it's easy enough to scare them from their hiding place before you've even found it. Just one little sentence to force them into the light. Three. Two. One.

"Ah ha!" I shouted. "I SEE YOU!"

It didn't matter that I had no idea where he was. All that mattered was he believed I could see him. From across the landing - the bedroom at the far end - Johnny screamed and ran from one room to the other (the bathroom) where he slammed the door shut. I heard the lock bolt across. Silly boy. He's only making this harder on himself.

"Fe-Fi-Fo-Fum...I smell the blood of a soon-to-be-screamin- in-agony little shit-faced cunt!" Not quite the words known, but good enough. I stomped loudly down the landing all the way to the door and tried the handle, despite knowing he had it locked. It didn't move. I rattled it backwards and forwards as he screamed from within. "Little shit, little shit, let me in..." I threw my weight against the door (he screamed again), shoulder first, in the hope I'd fall straight through. No such luck but there was definite movement. It won't take too much before it gives. I threw myself again the wooden door again, to the sound of yet another shriek from beyond. Scream all you want, kiddo; help isn't coming. A third slam against the wall, a four and fifth. On the sixth hit, the door finally gave in and I fell through, landing on the floor with a hard bang. Had it not been for the adrenaline - and the reward of getting in - that could have hurt. I looked up from the floor and saw the boy standing in the empty bath, clutching onto the shower curtain as though it were enough to stop me. Damn it. Foiled by a shower curtain. I don't fucking think so. I stood up to my full height and smiled at the boy. "Did you not hear me knocking?" I asked. I held the knife up and he screamed. I do wish he'd stop screaming. Little children should be seen and not heard. To his credit, he didn't try and run past me. He remained rooted to the spot, shaking like a leaf. I squeezed the handle of the knife tighter in my grip and took a deep breath in before...

These are the moments I live for.

These are the moments which make me feel alive.

The build-up.

The anticipation.

I thrust forward and penetrated the child's stomach with the knife to the accompaniment of the loudest scream I think I've ever heard. I'm unsure whether it is the boy or...whether it is him, crying into my ear. I twisted the knife deep in his intestines. No way that's going to seal itself back up again when I pull the knife out. No way he will survive the attack. Another scream from he who must be ignored as I stabbed the boy again, slightly to the side of the last hit.

IV

I looked away from the scene as he pulled the knife from Johnny's gut and thrust forward again. The poor child sounded as though he was in so much pain as he fell back against the wall. Out of the corner of my eye, I saw him slowly slide down into a sitting position, clutching his wounds as blood poured out from the gaping holes. I can't watch. I won't watch.

"What are you doing?" He sounded surprised that I was able to look away without much resistance. To be honest, I too was surprised. "Don't you fucking look away!" he yelled.

V

I snapped his head back to the boy, who was pale and gasping for air. It's my favourite bit, getting to see the life slowly slip away from the children. They make their parents suffer with their whining and constant demands - now it is my turn to make them suffer for as long as they're able to stand it (which is never usually that long). I thrust into his stomach with my white gloved hand - my fingers closed together and palm flat as though in a karate chop position. He's so near death now that he barely registered what I was doing. My hand was in his stomach. I opened my fingers up, stretching him wide, and took a hold of intestine. I smiled as I took a handful and slowly started pulling them from his gut. His body shook as I did so and his eyes rolled to the back of his head. A final gasp, like a fish out of water, and he stopped moving - at least stopping moving on his own accord. His body was still twitching due to my continued pulling out of his insides.

I've never done this before. They slipped to the floor with a watery slosh sound. Not sure why I've never thought to do it before. I have to say, that was pretty satisfying.

"You're a monster!" he was weeping in my ear. He tried to look away from my handiwork but I wouldn't let him. I wanted him to watch. I wanted him to see. This is me. This is us. And it's only going to get worse as the day and night progress.

I'm excited.

12

I should have done this at night for maximum impact for the father - the hero - Colin. I wanted him to walk into the living room illuminated with candlelight but it was too bright outside. Even with their curtains shut, daylight still managed to leak into the room. I had dragged both bodies into the living room - the mother and the boy. I'd sprawled them out on the floor by the unlit fireplace.

In my head, everything was so much better. Daddikins would come home, call out for them and there'd be no answer. He'd walk into the living room, eventually, and there he'd see them, propped up with their lifeless eyes staring straight into his own soul. The reality was much different and - compared to how it should have worked out - a little disappointing. The bodies wouldn't sit up properly. Every time I tried to make them, they'd just topple over. Worse yet, I had managed to spill so much blood from each body when I dragged them through to the living room that I had left a long trail of gore, enough of a mess for him to spot it as soon as he walked through the front door. Total lack of surprise, gone.

"You're a fucking monster."

He was still sulking with me. Had barely said anything to me whilst I was dragging the bodies around. Just the odd whimper here and there as he tried to hold his shit together. Fucking pathetic.

"I thought you'd left me," I sneered at him.

"I wish I could."

"As do I. At least we agree on that, hey."

"Fuck you."

"Don't worry," I told him, "the night will soon be over and all of this will be nothing but a distant memory...Unless, of course, it haunts you every night whilst you're locked in your little cell...Ooh, I can't imagine that will be too good for your precious little conscience."

I expected him to snap back at me but - to his credit - he remained silent. Probably saving his strength for the moment he is faced with the police so he can protest his innocence loudly enough to be heard. Little does he know, I won't let him. We're both going down for this. We're both going to prison. I won't let doctors psychoanalyse either of us. I won't let them take him off the sharp hook I have so skill-fully impaled him on. Fuck that.

With the bodies in place and the curtains shut, I took a hold of the knife again. The blade was filthy so I wiped it upon my suit until it was once again glistening. There. As good as new.

"Do you think he'll still love his wife?" I asked, as I looked at the pale body of a once mediocre-looking woman. "Or do you think he'll find her ugly now that she's dead? I've often wondered that. If you go through your whole life loving someone, if they die... Do they suddenly become ugly..."

"You're fucking insane."

"Of the two of us, my friend, I'd say that was you." I paused a moment, "But what do you think? Do you think he will still love her or...Did that love fade with her last breath?"

"I don't fucking know."

"You see - I only ask because - I was wondering whether you'd like one last fuck with her whilst she is still kind of warm. Get it in one final time before joining her in the bowels of Hell..."

"What makes you think they're in Hell?"

"Why wouldn't they be in Hell?" I asked.

Silence.

"I might give him the choice. Maybe it's your influence but...I have to say...I'm feeling a little generous."

"Then let him go. Take us home. We can pack a bag and just disappear. Talk things through. Work things out between us..."

"Shut the fuck up. You're like a broken record."

We both froze when we heard a key slide into the front door's lock.

"Please don't," he whispered, "we can still get away..."

"I'm home!" a male voice called from the hallway. It sounded like Colin - which was to be expected. "Honey? What the hell has happened here?" he shouted. And there goes the element of surprise. He's spotted the pooling of the blood from where his wife's body was slumped. "Susie?" he called out.

I didn't bother hiding myself. I just stood there, a proud look on my face, waiting by the bodies of his family members. One dead wife and one dead son to go, please.

"Susie?"

I took a step back to the mantlepiece above the fire and purposefully knocked one of the many pictures from it. It crashed to the floor. Only did it because I'm fucking bored of waiting for the cunt to come in here.

"Susie?"

Colin stepped into the room. He immediately spotted me. Second up - he saw his wife and child. His expression. He didn't know what to make of it. He was just standing there with his mouth agape. Say something. Show me some kind of reaction. He fidgeted on his feet. I could tell he didn't know what direction to go - whether to charge me or whether to run from the house.

"If you want to say goodbye to her body before you join her soul, she's still a little warm. But only if you fancy it," I offered. A kind offer. Generous. Is...he...turning me into a fucking faggot all of a sudden? Next up I'll be offering mercy. I laughed. Will I fuck.

"Wh-what...What is this?" Colin backed up slightly.

"Home invasion I guess. Nothing better to do." I raised the knife up so he could see it, "So what's it to be? Fancy having a good goodbye session with your wife or...Shall we just get on with this?"

Colin - the Hero of the Hour - started to cry like a baby. He dropped to his knees and wept. Well, I have to be honest, I expected a little more of a fight than this. Nearly as much of a pussy as he is.

"What the fuck are you doing?" I shouted at him. "What, you're not even going to try and fight? Not even going to try and get revenge? You're just going to kneel there like a fucking pussy?"

II

He was blinded by his own rage. I seized the opportunity and chucked the knife towards Colin. It landed to the side of him.

"Please!" I shouted. "KILL ME!"

Colin looked at the knife and then looked at me. Yes. That's it. Do it.

"What the FUCK are you doing?" he screamed in my ear as he took a step forward in an effort to take back the blade. I stopped him and we stumbled onto our knees. Colin reached over and grabbed a hold of the knife but still didn't rush us. Please. Come on. You have to do it. Quickly.

"I can't hold him back much longer!" I cried out. "Please! Kill me!"

Colin dragged himself up but still didn't rush forward. What the hell was his problem?

"Put that fucking knife down, you cunt!" he shouted at Colin.

"Shut up!" I shouted him down. "We deserve this."

"You do. I don't."

I turned to Colin, "We killed your family! KILL US!"

Colin screamed and rushed towards us with the blade held out in front of him. Yes. That's it. Come on. Do it. Stick that blade in me! Put me out of my fucking misery and end his life. Please!"

III

As Colin neared, I took control of the situation and jumped up. In the blink of an eye, I managed to grab Colin's hands and turn the knife back onto The Hero of the Hour. Using his own weight and momentum from his sudden rush towards me against him, I shoved it right into his gut. His eyes widened just as his wife's eyes did. Colin put his hands up to my throat and started to squeeze as I continued to twist the knife in his stomach. His grip didn't hurt. He was already starting to weaken. I laughed as I twisted the blade again. Not just because his efforts to hurt me were extremely amusing but - also - because of how we ended in this position.

"That's fucking team work, right?" I laughed.

He wasn't laughing though. He was screaming in my ear. He was screaming - calling me a 'murderer', a 'monster' - all the names under the sun. Some temper he has there but the name calling didn't bother me. For the first time in as long as I could remember, I felt as though we had bonded. Properly. And, more importantly, I'd shown him how easy it is to kill. The shouting was just for show. I bet - deep down - he fucking loved helping me put the blade in. Fucking loved it as much as I did. Maybe he'd get a taste for it? One thing seeing it, quite another doing it yourself (or at least having a helping hand in it). Maybe we could still run from here and live a life killing who and what we wanted? My mind was flowing with various plans on how we could get away with living a life like this…The two of us…

IV

I grabbed for the knife and pulled it from the father's stomach. With no hesitation I turned it back on myself and rammed it straight back into my chest until it was up to its handle. Surprisingly, I felt no pain. I felt nothing. It wasn't my chest. It was his chest. We dropped to our knees, the pair of us gasping for breath. He took a hold of the handle and pulled the blade from our chest and dropped it to the floor. I sensed he was trying to say something to me. No doubt trying to call me a fucking idiot or words to that effect but I didn't care. Didn't give a shit. I just watched the blood flow freely from the hole he'd left behind by removing the blade.

Our legs feel cold.

I feel sleepy.

Not sure where I managed to find the strength to do this but…I'm glad.

We slumped forward, face first, onto the family's cream carpet. The blood was soaking in. Not sure whether it's the family's blood or my own blood…Doesn't matter.

Really sleepy.

I smiled.

It's peaceful here.

V

I snorted. Too weak to laugh. Didn't see it coming. Have to admit.

I couldn't keep my eyes open. My eyelids slowly closed. Can't open them again.

I can't believe he killed us.

What...

...A

...Cunt.

T H E   E N D

Printed in Great Britain
by Amazon